SPACES   LIKE   STAIRS

SPACES LIKE STAIRS

Essays

by

GAIL SCOTT

The
Women's
·Press·

CANADIAN CATALOGUING IN PUBLICATION DATA

Scott, Gail
Spaces like stairs

ISBN 0-88961-131-9

1. Scott, Gail. 2. Feminism and literature.
3. Authorship. 4. Women authors, Canadian
(English) – Quebec (Province) – Biography.*
I. Title.

PS8587.C623S68 1989   C818'.5409   C89-093887-3
PR9199.3.S35S68 1989

Cover art by Barbara Steinman
(Detail: *Borrowed Scenery,* multimedia installation, 1987)
Cover design: Linda Gustafson
Editor: Marlene Kadar
Copy editor and proofreader: Margaret Christakos

Published by
The Women's Press
229 College Street, No. 204
Toronto, Ontario M5T 1R4

This book was produced by
the collective effort of members of
The Women's Press.
This book was a project of the Translation Group.
The Women's Press gratefully acknowledges
financial support from The Canada Council
and the Ontario Arts Council
Printed and bound in Canada

1   2   3   4   5   1992   1991   1990   1989

CONTENTS

ACKNOWLEDGEMENTS

Some of the following texts have appeared, usually in earlier versions, in *Room of One's Own (Tessera)*, *Canadian Fiction Magazine (Tessera)*, *Canadian Forum*, *Brick*, *Trivia*, and *la nouvelle barre du jour*.

"Shaping A Vehicle For Her Use" was anthologized in *in the feminine: women and words / les femmes et les mots, Conference Proceedings, 1983*, ed. Ann Dybikowski et al (Edmonton: Longspoon Press, 1985).

"Virginia And Colette: On The Outside Looking In" was anthologized in *A Mazing Space: Writing Canadian Women Writing*, ed. Shirley Neuman and Smaro Kamboureli (Edmonton: Longspoon / Newest, 1986).

"A Feminist at the Carnival" appeared, in a translation by Claudine Vivier, in *La Théorie, un dimanche*, by Nicole Brossard, Louky Bersianik, Louise Cotnoir, Louise Dupré, Gail Scott and France Théoret (Montréal: Les Editions du remue-ménage, 1988).

I would like to thank Marlene Kadar for her sensitive and informed editing. (And Marlene and Rona Moreau for suggesting this book to me.)

PREFACE

An essay is a perpetual work-in-progress. I like the immediacy of this: the way an essay (even more than fiction) precisely intersects the period in which it is written. The way it is marked, at a given moment, by its context, its community, both of which are also part of how the writer is and how she changes over time.

I say "marked" rather than dated in homage to writers like Virginia Woolf who, although writing decades ago, reassured me and others that our discomfort with the novel form, or the sentence, was not proof of our incompetence. "To begin with ... the very form of the sentence does not fit her," said Woolf. "It is a sentence made by men, too loose, too heavy, too pompous for a woman's use." Some of what Woolf wrote also indicated points where her vision rubbed against, was contained by her context, her time: for example, her counsel (which she herself did not heed in her fiction) that the woman author maintain a safe distance from the feminine. "The aloofness," she wrote, "that was once within the reach of genius and originality is ... now coming within the reach of ordinary women." But these limits are instructive, too, offering at the very least a record of how, as women, our ideas about writing are evolving.

To write about how we write, then, is to try and understand the processes of our work, to share with others a record of what we have grasped (our breakthroughs) and of what we have failed to grasp (our limits). Perhaps I should say, instead, it is a record of the movement of our writing, writing pushing on the edges of the blanks in discourse, the gaps in history, the spaces between the established genres of a male-dominant literary canon—which remind us of our exclusion, to varying degrees, as women.

What is political about this is the *we*. The following essays emerge (among others) from a network of women speaking, writing, thinking. In fact, they intersect a decade of remarkable flowering of feminist, postmodern writing in Québec—a decade where the ethical function of the text has been underscored in a writing practice greatly concerned with deciphering the effects of social constructs in language. This emphasis on the relationship between our struggles and writing-as-change has gained us, I believe, a new sense of what the essay is: a form deriving not only from the ideological, but also, the self-reflexive and the fictional. In other words, a text where the everyday, the political, the cultural meet, risking syntax in the process of positing and dissolving "meaning" (notably the traces of male dominance), and the (traditional female) subject.

Our concern with language, syntax, as a collective issue has also liberated us from an overdetermined deference to academic authority when it comes to theory. It is significant theoretically as well as politically (i.e., in terms of feminist practice), that the work of analyzing our own fictional processes has been largely outside the academy, albeit intensely (but critically) informed by modernity.* Many of the following texts, for example, have been written for public or private discussions among feminist writers, or for special issues of literary periodicals. Our writing-about-writing is also about women occupying a space usually left to an "interpretive milieu" of critics and the academy—a milieu of great importance to us, but whose own particular agenda isn't always ours....

These essays / texts do not, therefore, make firm statements about writing in-the-feminine. They are, simply, (and not so simply) the story of a writer's journey among the literary, theoretical, political signposts of a certain period (the late 70s and 80s) in a certain place (Québec). I have altered some of the previously published texts considerably for style. But I have resisted the temptation to alter positions, or at least nuances, in the earlier texts that may differ from what I think now. (Notably, my notion of how writing might uncover a "self" in-the-feminine has altered over time.) For to do so would also be to edit out a heady sense of discovery, occasionally naïve, perhaps, but which also reflected the ambience of the period in which each of these essays was written.

Indeed, most complex for me, most exciting, too, in developing this work, is the job of imagining what I now think of as a "writing subject" in-the-feminine. Not the "self" as a (feminist or otherwise) predetermined figure, but a complex tissue of texts, experience, evolving in the very act of writing. We have learned from forerunners like Woolf, as well as from contemporary struggles, that our alienation within sexist language / cultural practices starts from the fact that we are writing from the socially marginalized feminine. There has further been, among contemporary writers, an insistence that we, who have been muted and mocked, write from this feminine space with an exploratory, even caressing, rather than an "objectifying," hand. But the space the writing enters, attempts to decipher, is both the space of modernity (that fluid space of meaning constantly taken apart, deferred), and a space infused with our desire for a female subject-in-process. We know that the hand that guides the pen—and the culture in which that text will be "received"—are influenced by race, sex, class. We also know that the intersection of language (lovingly, consciously used, word by word) within the space of a (con)text is a continuously shifting, poetic project. As if a word written across a space—even a space we have "appropriated" thanks to our feminist consciousness—must immediately give way to another. So the spaces unroll around us. Like stairs . . .

* I have often used "modernity" instead of "postmodernism" in these texts, partly because the term, a direct translation of the French *modernité*, underscores the importance of contemporary French influence on women of my generation writing in Québec. I also like the fact that "modernity" evokes a practice consistently involved with questioning ideological assumptions.

1

MOI ET L'AUTRE

RED TIN + WHITE TULLE
ON MEMORY AND WRITING

What of writing and the body? Not the body as object, to be observed, described, but the body as pulsion, rhythm, and ... vehicle of memory. In the late 70s, the idea that we might rupture patriarchal fictions by letting what we heard / sensed of our female bodies spill over into a new kind of writing seemed dazzlingly subversive. Yet, as I read Cixous and other new French feminists, I felt a strangeness: a feeling my relationship to my body might be different than theirs. I began to think about how one's body is not only gendered, but is also linguistic, cultural, economic. So the question for me became, what of the relationship between writing and the rhythms, pulsions, memories of my Protestant body . . . mediated by an English-language inscription in-the-feminine?

I tried to confront that question as the only woman from a Protestant background at a retreat of Québécois feminist writers in New Brunswick in August, 1980. To confront "body"— especially as a vehicle of memory. I couldn't have found a more ideal situation to start this reflection. There was, of course, a tremendous sense of collegiality among us. We worked intensely in groups in the morning, in the large wood-paneled livingroom of Stanley House on the Bay of Fundy. We wrote in the afternoon, and for breaks, took walks in the surrounding woods. Or continued our talks on the beach. As summer was waning, the cool weather often created mist on the bay, which was shallow and had plenty of herons. I remember lying on the sand, feeling the presence of the other women's bodies, listening to the resonance of their French-speaking voices.

MEMORY: THE SKULL rattle of coke cans under the wedding car.

But why this marriage symbol? Followed by a skull rattle? The immediate paranoia. Coke cans, not as in cool drinks. But as in signs of oft-polluting technology on faroff desert sands. And under the wedding car.

A *woman's* memory then. Unwinding back to double-sided images: "truth" plus fiction. Red tin + white tulle. Easily torn. Yet, can't say so because the wedding is a ceremony of mirth. Hence, the unwinding of words, the thinking back, (language ... the true practice of thought)[1] leading to . . . the inexpressible. The inexpressible pain of contradiction. Unless, behind it all somewhere, perhaps in an ocean-crevice of madness, lies the simple, undeniable lucidity: "I see the fish swimming deep in the sea," says the stoned Mexican skindiver. "They are beautiful colours. And do you know something? They are kissing."

I used to live in a triangle. Mother, God and me. At night, when I felt abandoned by my lovers, betrayed by my friends, I prayed. To her. She was a ghost with penetrating eyes. She always said ... what mothers used to say: *"You don't know how to love."* Her discourse was toned guilty and resentful. But wait. What discourse? And whose inadequacy was she owning for herself, then passing on to me? Boy children are rarely criticized for an incapacity to love. No, in the mouths of mothers it's daughters who are responsible for the affective parsimony of patriarchal culture. In my case, the Protestant version. Just an example of how language is twisted into its opposite, so our own meanings are often hidden from us.[2] We may use language our whole lives without noticing the distortions.

Distortions and omissions. Surely the assertion of the inner self has to start with language. But what if the surfacing unconscious stream finds void instead of code? What if we often

17

lack the facility to raise to the conscious level our unconscious thoughts?[3] Due to our slant relationship with culture, therefore language, the words won't come. And without the words, the self. No capacity for separation.

Ottawa, 1962. I lie in bed with my bathing suit on. Too hot. Too cold. Now too hot. Very still. My knees drawn up in a hump. My mother taking her Sunday afternoon nap. The Sunday roast hardens in the oven.[4]

Mother and me. Simulated in the same skin. The vicious-circle search for boundaries in the memory-mass of borrowed phrases. Like and dislike. Her warmth. Her (frightened) love. Her (my) inadequate breast. Under the padded bra. The hard roast. Females incompetent at being female in a culture where the feminine is . . . muted. But is there any culture where it isn't? Their judgements fill our silence. "Women are muted because men are in control, and the language, and the meanings, and the knowledge of women cannot be accounted for outside that control."[5]

Across the street, Véronique Paquette walks by terriblement décolletée. The priest gives her shit every Sunday, but she still does it just the same. 'Frogs,' says my father, one of the three bank managers, all brothers. Drunkenly they flex their lip muscles at her from where they sit in their rocking chairs on the prairie. Then he looks up at me sitting on the verandah and shouts 'Get your nose back in that Bible, it's Sunday.[6] Sex and ethnicity. Double and indivisible chauvinism.

Mother wouldn't be seated on the prairie. She'd be upstairs

sleeping, on account of her exhaustion. I imagine a slogan on
the wall: "Harmony in the family keeps order in the nation."
Her knees drawn up in defence against the terrible task that
homily would impose. The knees again. I am she taking our
Sunday afternoon nap. Now she's gone I carry her inside as
she once carried me. Trying to understand the effect of her
all-seeing eyes, socketed in the steeple of Protestant funda-
mentalism. The love for her. The hate. Separation would have
to be by assault. Yet, her unspoken frustrations also formed
the warp of my rebellion. So that once I had ripped off that
outer nagging, fearful fictional mask of the mother, I found a
troubled strength. And the desire to recreate her as a kind of
strange, almost gothic, heroine.

But: can a modern woman writing admit to an imagination
peopled with images that are so ... weird? And why have I, for
this text with its theoretical intention, transformed these
images from *my* memory into something even more fictional
and carnivalesque? As if there were no line between autobiography and romanesque. The slogans on the wall, for example,
weren't at home, but on the wall of a real Orange Hall I saw on
a trip to Newfoundland. Visiting the outports there, I was
astonished at how the small towns resembled the Eastern
Ontario village where I grew up. With the hard lines drawn,
the sense of separate worlds for Protestant and Catholic:
Irish-Catholic there; French-Catholic in my village. And like
back home, there were not only the different kinds of steeples
to go with different kinds of thinking. But also all-male groups
to militantly protect those "for Rome" and those against it:
Knights of Columbus, Orangemen and Masons. In summers,
the Orangemen would arrogantly parade the streets on huge
white horses, while well behind, small French boys clowned,
perhaps to hide a kind of collective consternation. At home,
my father packed a funny apron before going off to Masons.

"You're exaggerating," said the young man with whom I
walked from cove to cove, from bay to bay, on that New-

foundland vacation. "Religion's dead. The differences between Protestant and Catholic don't matter any longer. For my
generation anyway," he added, teasingly, since I was ten years
older. Yes, the icons in my mind reflected having grown up in
a family not only Protestant, but also exceedingly religious.
But (I told him), most people growing up in cultures where
Protestantism is an aspect of the dominant ideology end up
with certain common attitudes springing from that Protestant
source regarding honour, love, authority, the family, etc. And
women. Even if they never go to church. For memory, a
many-sided fiction, serves up different types of images—often
strongly coded ideologically—to reflect the "real."

Still, there was some truth in what he said. Certain images
from my rural childhood, men on white horses and women
exhausted (yet also strengthened, "uplifted") by the effects of
those fundamentalist slogans, did seem provincial, to say the
least. Perhaps (I thought), as a modernist and a feminist, I
should not treat memory as merely the play of random
thought, producing circus-like processions, sometimes
happy, sometimes troubling. Their nature depending on my
mood, my context at the time. Rather, I should be more consciously, more intellectually selective in the process of choos-
ing memories with which to work.

Yes, this was better, this idea of creating a conspiracy
between remembering and one's desire to move forward.
Example, the issue of women's need to identify with positive
female others. One might, in this instance, displace the memory category of mothers (so often negative, restricted, unac-
complished professionally) to . . . literary mothers. Margaret
Atwood could be a model. Except (comes this nagging,
hypercritical voice inside me) many of her women characters
are so ... grim. Take Elizabeth in *Life Before Man*.... But wait.
Why is my seeking out of *like* immediately coupled with a
desire to distance through attack? As if any "mother-figure"
must be chronically in the wrong. Yet (here's the double

bind), Atwood seems to have this same negative attitude towards her character Elizabeth. Example, Elizabeth is responsible for the affective lack in her domestic situation. While husband Nate is soft and sentimental. (The sympathizer of oppressed Québec as well.) He wants to reach out to her. But she is too rigid to respond. Uptight. Can't give. Doesn't know how to love. Translate *live*. The woman's fault?

I prefer Colette. Longing, often, when I read the women novelists of my culture, for a more sensual rapport between writer and her female subjects: for more soft cheeks, for the gracious curves of arms. Longing perhaps for writing that shows its love for women, hence for self as female. Or maybe, longing to close the gap between mind and (female) body: in a sense, that space between narrator and story in the English novel as we know it. Longing to "write with the body," to use an expression current (in 1980) in Québec. Except the question of body (pleasure) is somehow hard in English. "In English, we have either the coarse or the clinical, and by tradition our words for our pleasures, even for the intimate parts of our bodies where we may take these pleasures, come awkwardly when they come at all," notes the introduction to the English translation of Roland Barthes' *The Pleasure of the Text*.[7]

In the childhood image, God is inside. So you can't confess. He sees everything. That's Protestantism. Does the relationship to "sin" (the lack of a confessional, a process of atonement to relieve the guilt) affect a woman's relationship to her body? I wonder if women from Catholic-dominant cultures have the same overwhelming sense of the male deity (in its symbolic sense) inside? Maybe there was some mixed blessing in his being accompanied in the Church window by the feminine face of Mary. Maybe the loss of that last feminine symbol, incarnated, it's true, in the prissy image of a virgin mother, cost Protestant women something in terms of increasing degradation of "feminine" qualities and values.[8] So we end up feeling like poor replicas of a disappearing memory. *"What I wanted was a natural woman"* (whatever that is!). Words from a popular song of the late 60s. Spender says: "In language female gender is not natural."[9]

And what then of the body/language tandem in our English-speaking women's writing? When second-wave feminists first began to explore the problems of women in patriarchy, I often heard it said the English language was neutral, requiring only minor changes to make it adequate for our use. But as we struggled to express ourselves in language, as well as in the new lives we were forging for ourselves, there were problems. These problems we also experienced when working politically with men or talking to the media: we found ourselves constantly monitoring our language to be "clear." All of this is not surprising when one remembers that nineteenth-century grammarians decreed that in language the male gender is more comprehensive. Thus, the precedence of he and man (man shall not live by bread alone) over woman, making much of language androcentric. (The male gender is also comprehensive in French when both genders are implied; otherwise, unlike English, the feminine is signaled in verb endings, in adjectives.)

But if language is the real work of thinking, and if without memory (the thinking back) there can be no sense of self, where does that leave women? Speaking in tongues, no doubt: that is, not through our "own" voices. Is that why I resent the fictional representation of Atwood's Elizabeth as an ice-cold broad? My desire would have been to have her captured in a process of becoming, with critical attention to (her imagined) language, deciphering "her" words as they spilled on the page. So that I the reader might be able to see past her barrier of fear or guilt, perhaps find something deeper, or at least another side in her. Of course, this is another writing project, completely—based on my obsession with delving beneath the racket of patriarchal laws of economics, systems, as reflected in the surface of language. "The development of this hearing faculty and power of speech involves the dislodging of images that reflect and reinforce prevailing social arrangements," says Mary Daly.[10]

The contradiction is that in delving into memory by letting language take us where it will, we tend to uncover things we intended to repress....

The maple trees blew on the hot summer street. The little girl stepped off the curb. In her mind she wrote: "The little girl stepped off the curb." The little girl crossed the street. In her mind she wrote: "The little girl crossed the street." Lucinda McVitty, the old maid, was sitting on the verandah. The little girl did not write that the *old maid* was sitting on the verandah.

Again the language void in precisely the troubled spot. For what could that little girl, who knew she wanted to be a writer and maybe wouldn't marry, call the single older woman? Her mother was no help. It was okay to do well in school and get A in English composition. But she mustn't be a dreamer. A few years later (the early 60s), her mother asked her to answer a magazine quiz called *Are You Likely to Get Married?* Her score was mediocre. Her mother's eyes said: "You won't make it." Her mouth said: "You're too romantic."

This memory is embarrassing. But have things changed so much? Or have the symbols just transformed to trendier representations of the same thing? The Yuppie couple might focus less on the ceremony than on the snazzy car and condominium their combined salaries will buy. But I suspect their hopes are similar to those that lay behind the coupling symbols our mothers held out to us. Naturally, the security of tradition. And the element of safety conventional wisdom attributes to life inside the family. Perhaps, somewhat more positively, the link of certain feminine values with life and reproduction. As well, marriage provided Mother with a community of women, sisters, aunts, neighbours, in which those values could be safe from what Virginia Woolf called patriarchy's processions.

The "culture" she and other women of the family passed on to me included how to find the fattest raspberries on the underside of bushes. The taste of fresh trout at breakfast. How to smock a dress! A love of birds. And gardening. Stories, hymns, songs. As an adolescent I rejected them. In part because the life my mother and grandmother attempted to preserve as they sweated over cauldrons of wild berries or garden vegetables or pickles on grandma's gleaming wood stove (or in our apartment) was infused with a kind of sadness. They were both attentive to perfection, yet strangely absent as they swept floors, tended children, cooked, sewed. I have very little recollection of the presence of their bodies. As if some internal interdiction demanded (or was it the struggle between the patriarchal coding and some muted women's culture) that their physical presence be diminished. They both died young of cancer. Is their cancer-shrinking flesh the skull rattle I hear under the wedding car?

Memory: how it's received and written. When certain images are encoded, even as they surface, by the implicit patriarchal judgement of women embedded in the language. That silly wedding car: melodramatic, kitsch. We have two choices: to bury or confront them. And confronting means ... deconstructing them. Virginia Woolf frequently advocated breaking the sentence in order to overcome women's sense of awkwardness, inferiority in writing.[11] This is why writing focused on language (where words, syntax, are the real material of writing, not necessarily subjugated to genre requirements such as plot) is so important for feminists.

Memory, then, as a reconnaissance operation. A tool for writing, but not as mere description. "Je n'écris pas la mémoire, je la *travaille*," says a Québécois writer friend. This implies a double-sided movement: both opening the floodgates of possibility (letting the play of images, the writing be an exploration of the undersides of words); then imposing another kind of sentence (vision, rhythm) on them. If this new rhythm, order, is to go beyond patriarchal limits, it will no doubt have to be structured by feminist awareness. (In this sense, our postmodernism with its consciously female subject is quite different from that of men—where the subject is distanced, erased, or, "neuter."[12]) But what is important for me is the doubleness of the process: on one hand, the open floodgates, the permission to behave excessively, so we can't bury things or miss the point by failing to undo the contradictions that block the way to deeper cognizance. On the other hand, the presence (in a corner of our mind) of our own vision of utopia (where she / I can exist as a whole person) so we don't drown or tumble into despair. Perhaps, for feminist writers of the English-Protestant tradition, it's the horror of excess that is our greater fear. Who of us would dare to repeat Jovette Marchessault's marvelous declaration: "My mother is a cow."[13]

That's why when Nicole Brossard said: "the theme for the retreat is memory" and I got this old-fashioned image of red tin (the coke cans under the wedding car) + white tulle, I decided not to bury it but to trace it. My mother's fantasy of the wedding, reduced by me to the figure of a car, appears frequently in my stories. But displaced. So it's a getaway car. Not fleeing the wedding guests towards the legendary paradise of the honeymoon. Fleeing, rather, from the fear of the daughter repeating the mother's life. My love (for her) and my (self?) hate. *Le début du mépris.* The car carries women in search of light. But not quite free. One is driven by a cowboy. Another, carrying a mother and daughter involved in some kind of crazy search for female symbols is smashed in simulated rape (from behind) by . . . Elvis. The ambiguity that imbues the car represents a surface layer of images. Leading back, when worked on, to forgotten stories, meanings, that open new doors. Leading me down that proverbial garden path she always wanted me to stay off.

It seems so clear that, as women, we have been forced to operate in language from a negative semantic space, reduced or missing from the range of positive symbols. What choice do we have but to seize language and find new ways to use it? Getting in touch with our own rhythms, so different from the ticker-tape rhythm of the talking (media) world which constantly invades our consciousness. My writerly intuition tells me that part of the process is getting behind the cover of cultural ennui, skirting linguistic and legalistic conventions by asserting our feminine voice—a voice that may be initially denigrated as hysterical by some, self-indulgent, narcissistic by others. For it is not language itself, but the social conditions governing its use that pose the problem. Remember the wonderful elasticity of early English? We will proceed then, discovering the images behind the images, until we hear the tinkling laughter of Queen Titania (dim reflection of a murdered goddess)—who prefers an ass to her king.

This is not a question of our writing being focused on the past. I'm talking about finding the memory traces of the feminine in our present language, our present acts, our present sentences, our present lovemaking. Listening to our own voices and the speech patterns of women.

"As soon as we learn words we find ourselves outside them," British writer Sheila Rowbotham said somewhere.

But it isn't necessary. One just has to get over that fear of sounding . . . different.

Montréal, 1980

NOTES

1 Julia Kristeva, *Desire In Language: A Semiotic Approach to Literature and Art*, trans. Léon S. Roudiez, Alice Jardine and Thomas Gora (New York: Columbia University Press, 1980), p. 65.

2 Dale Spender, *Man Made Language* (London: Routledge & Kegan Paul, 1980), p. 145.

3 Ibid, p. 82, citing Shirley Ardener (ed.) in *Perceiving Women* (Malaby, 1975).

4 Gail Scott, *Spare Parts* (Toronto: Coach House Press, 1982), p. 27.

5 Spender, p. 77.

6 Scott, p. 49.

7 Roland Barthes, *The Pleasure of the Text*, trans. Richard Miller (New York: Farrar, Straus and Giroux, Inc., 1975), p. v.

8 Mary Daly deals with this question extensively in *Beyond God the Father: Towards a Philosophy of Women's Liberation* (Boston: Beacon Press, 1973).

9 Spender, p. 160.

10 Mary Daly, p. 10.

11 The need for women writers to assault the sentence was discussed by Virginia Woolf in *A Room of One's Own* and in "Women and Fiction" in the essay collection *Granite and Rainbow*.

12 According to Alice Jardine, Jacques Derrida never answers his own question about the eternal resemblance between the masculine *il* and the neuter *il*. He insists only on the need of a neuter for a "narrative" that would be "borne beyond the system of philosophical oppositions." In *Gynesis: Configurations of Women and Modernity* (Ithaca: Cornell University Press, 1986), p. 204.

13 Jovette Marchessault, "Night Cows," *Lesbian Triptych*, trans. Yvonne M. Klein (Toronto: Women's Press, 1985), p. 73.

VIRGINIA AND COLETTE: ON THE OUTSIDE LOOKING IN

Being a minority anglophone in a largely French milieu surely throws more light on one's own culture than on the culture of the other. In so doing, it offers ammunition for one of a writer's most important tasks: a constant, rigorous criticism of her nation's dominant culture. A corollary of this is that my very notion of fiction has been transformed by the fact that I happened to start writing seriously in a lieu culturally distanced from the realist tradition of strong English-Canadian women writers, a lieu where women were more concerned with syntax and language than with "story." In exploring this place I write from, an important reminiscence concerns my meeting France Théoret, and the intense writing relationship our common feminism permitted us to develop despite the mutually antagonistic rapport that existed between our respective national cultures (1976). When our gaze fixed on each other's culture it often brought about amusing inversals. For example, as we grew closer, I playfully projected on her the qualities of the great Colette, a writer whom I admired more than she did. And, sometimes, too, I took on for her what she called the "reassuring asceticism" of Virginia Woolf. We knew these projections were absurd, but they were a way of getting behind the masks of the ethnic reticences that were such an old story in both our cultures.

IT NEVER CEASES to amaze me how a concept bears within itself its own contradiction. The 70s "revolution" in Poland was Catholic in part, and this limited the debate on women's issues, among others, thus falling short of radical change. Marxism in its social and political manifestations has meant to date in many countries the freedom to eat at the cost of the freedom to speak. I have seen the *circus side* of the Nazi phenomenon described as a need for ritual, pomp and ceremony such as that present in the rites of Catholicism, breaking through the bland, repressive surface of German Protestantism. In Canada being French or English is more than a concept, of course: historically it's a conviction that contains at its core the attraction-repulsion attitude towards the other that is both at the root of racism and of certain *grandes passions*. The other is what we lack—or fear we lack—in self.

For women, the (masculine) other is often seen as the way out of self, and the way back to self—that self which has been amputated, refused by patriarchy, that self struggling to be made whole. We know that self is beyond the narcissistic image of what is "feminine"—so jealously maintained by culture to keep us down. The way out is dangerous, however, because of the temptation, so strongly implanted, of self-hate, of total rejection of the image we see in the mirror as we reach for something that stands behind it. In a gesture of transferal I make that second image into my cultural opposite. I know she is also an illusion. But I must have that illusion for it represents the lack I feel in myself.

France-Colette. Our meeting was prepared a long time in advance. We had grown up in the shadow of each other's culture, seduced by what we saw from afar. The discoveries we made in the process of growing closer (we met shortly after the 1976 victory of the Parti Québécois) were as much discoveries about ourselves as discoveries about the other.

The confrontation of our cultures, of our culturally different versions of feminism, facilitated for each of us the un-making of our respective mythologies—that is the mythologies with which we were each shouldered as female children growing up in the 50s. "If we exist anywhere," said France, "it must be as women of our generation." What we had in common was the social schizophrenia of two women straddling a transitional epoch. Rock 'n' roll interspersed with square dancing was what we both did on Saturday night.

Happiness, said Colette, is merely a matter of changing troubles.[1] Slightly modified, the definition could be applied to the question of female identity. There are no role models. Life, like literature, is a matter of plagiarizing and cutting up. What is significant is what we choose to hear. What I hear in Colette that aids and abets me in my feminist desire to "subvert" Protestantism. What France hears in the English Virginia. What France and I heard during the late 70s in each other's discourse, in each other's texts, in each other's approach to feminism. What we have heard that has irrevocably altered our relationship to our writing.

I wonder if men could listen the way we have? Our pores were always open, for we were used to being defined by others: one of the first lessons little girls learn. The beginning of *l'excentrement du je,* the un-centred self, prepared and reinforced by the repression of the little girl's libido. *"C'est au fond, en petit homme, que la fillette aime sa mère,"*[2] says Luce Irigaray. But the little man or little being is never allowed to exist as herself, for herself.

The product of such an education cannot but have a chancy relationship to culture, regardless of the language in which it is mediated. A certain cynicism must lurk behind the face constantly striving to adapt to the reflection of self it sees in the eye of the other. Imagine an over-sensitive girl, the child of

white imperialists, growing up acutely aware of the image she
and her kind project in the eyes of the indigenous population.
With what clarity she perceives the ugliness of her own
greedy "civilization." It is perhaps no accident that two of the
women writers most admired by Western culture grew up in
precisely such circumstances: Doris Lessing and Marguerite
Duras.

"Nothing gives more assurance than a mask."[3] Colette
again. Without doubt, for women, adopting the posture of the
writer is dangerously close to wearing a mask, to adapting to
an image invented by the masculine other. For the role models
are largely male. Yet the circumstances of our everyday lives
make it difficult to say with the confidence of a Claude Beausoleil: *"Pour moi, la neige, à la limite, est plus abstraite que le
texte."*[4] Our relationship to language, to literature, where
tastes and standards are set by male-dominant culture, is distanced by the million little details of everyday life as wife,
lover, mother. Finding the two-year-old's mittens, for
example, gives that snow a concrete edge. To live and breathe
literature, one must be able to *se garder au-dessus de la mêlée,*
something Joyce apparently did with great success despite
family illness, terrible financial problems, etc. For a man such
ivory-tower solitude by no means implies that he lives alone.
But for a woman, demanding the conditions that would permit a fervent, never-ceasing relationship to *le texte* conjures up
the image of the crochety eccentric, she who refuses the many
small labours necessary for seduction, for the nurturing of
other humans. Lesbians, through the sharing of nurturing,
avoid this dilemma to some extent—which may explain why
much of the twentieth century's best writing by women is, in
fact, by lesbians. Paradoxically, this has not improved
society's attitudes towards women who love women.

The discussion about the relationship between the conditions of women's lives and formal research in writing began in
Québec in the mid-70s with the appearance of the feminist

periodical *Têtes de Pioche*. The air was afire with ideas, ideas
that corresponded to my own struggles with writing. The
problem for me was my desire to break the fictional line when
I wrote. For me, that linear movement did not correspond to
the way we think, talk, live. I was looking for a relationship
between my need to "explode" language, syntax and what I
perceived as my fractured female ego. I was also fascinated by
how desire circulated through the masks that my women
friends and I seemed to adopt in our various roles: mother,
writer, militant, lover, friend. This seemed to preclude the
development of unary female characters in prose, and consequently, of plot in any conventional sense. I was intrigued by
Luce Irigaray's circular vision of things in her book *Ce Sexe qui
n'en est pas un* (1977). The desire of women, she contended,
does not speak the same language as that of men, but it has
been covered over by male logic since the Greeks. Later this
idea became, more clearly, writing across the absence that
Nicole Brossard had already prophetically called *Le Centre
blanc*.[5]

This emphasis on language in writing (called *la modernité*
in Québec) and its rapport with feminist struggle was at the
core of the nurturing literary relationship between France
Théoret and me. The recurring question for us was how we
stood as women vis-à-vis language and culture in a patriarchal
society. And, for me, there was a corollary question: how was
this stance coloured by our respective English and French
backgrounds. In her famous essay on women's writing, "The
Laugh of the Medusa," Hélène Cixous talks of "female-sexed"
texts: "There is not that ... scission," she says of women's writing, "made by the common man between the logic of oral
speech and the logic of the text, bound as he is by his anti-
quated relation ... to mastery. From which proceeds the lip-
service which engages only the tiniest part of the body, plus
the mask."[6]

Reading Cixous' essay was one of several factors in that

heady period which dissolved any desire I had to attempt writing fiction in traditional forms. But there was also the thorny problem that the feminine persona that emerged from Cixous' pages, passionately throwing her body into her speech when, for example, she addressed a public meeting, was not a figure of Anglo-Protestantism. To what extent was I different from her? Should I try and put a value judgement on that difference, i.e., was I culturally more alienated from my physical self (as female) than she was? (Or was this another male cliché?) And what did it mean in terms of my writing? France and I began talking in earnest, often regretting after that we had failed to record our discussions. For we had embarked on a process of lifting masks, of shifting the images of self and other that were the clichés of our respective pasts.

My first meeting with France was in a St. Denis St. café. Her beret was at a cocky angle, her smile warm as she pushed her poems across the table. No doubt I was projecting on her at that moment my image of Colette: a total presence; an intelligence both sensual and cerebral. At the same time France was probably projecting on me what she called the "reassuring asceticism" of Virginia Woolf. But even as we articulated the stereotyped image of the other, we mocked it. There began a strange game of mirrors. For what we thought we saw in the other was often what was trying to emerge in ourselves.

One of the images I carry in my head of what it means to be English is something akin to the Salvation Army, rigid and faintly ridiculous. Where does it come from? No doubt partly from my childhood: those endless Sunday afternoons, when Mother, who was religious, took a dim view of any Sunday activity that might be *fun*. I sat on the verandah watching the French kids across the street—with their dog Bijou, their elder sister in her high heels and make-up, their music, their laughing—watch me. Already I was aware of standing outside not only the other but also the image of self projected by the other. Yet I was aware also that I was not the figure of the young girl represented by the conventions of my own culture. France, too, who frowns at my fondness for Catholic rite, stood in a similar relationship to her culture. "The feast is hypocrisy," she says, "the better to mask the moralism."

Yes, religion. The masks of self and other represented by French and English quickly gave way to reveal another reality: that of religion—or at least the ideological and symbolic heritage of growing up Catholic or Protestant. Admittedly, clearing that first small hurdle of nation was in itself no small matter. Not only was the weight of our respective national histories with us, but also our childhood memories of Eastern Ontario and Québec in the 50s. In the half-French village where I grew up, the English spoke of "the French" with disparagement, forcing on them a hundred humiliations, including the refusal of French-language high schools. Thus, the French students, unable to cope in a second language, often ended their schooling after grade nine. For France, there was the Montréal convent where small Catholic girls were warned of the dire (spiritual?) consequences of entering a Protestant house. I'm sure the barrier of nation was harder for France to hurdle than it was for me. She was part of a culture that was boiling with anger. But two factors, I think, made it easier: first, the 1976 victory of the Parti Québécois, an important step in reclaiming national pride; and secondly, the intensity of our feminism, which made us impatient to understand our past, the better to break with it.

Religion. What it, through its input into ideology, has done to each of us. I remember a discussion we had about Michel Tremblay's novel *Thérèse et Pierrette à l'école des Saints-Anges.*[7] My feminism bristled at the monstrous picture Tremblay paints of the nuns. In it I saw just one more misogynist plot to put down the few women in Québec who had gained any access to the professions. Perhaps it rubbed too close to the anti-Catholic image of the sisters as punitive birds with which I was raised in our Protestant household. (There was a paper pinned on the kitchen wall. If I got ten black marks on that paper for bad behaviour I would be sent to a convent. The fate, as it was described to me, was infinitely worse than jail.) France protests at my objections to Tremblay, "But the nuns *were* like that," she says. Quickly, however, it was the symbolic implications of religion that became the focal point of our discussions.

What struck me again, talking to France, was the lack of female figures in Protestant iconography. Was this not symbolic of the repression of female values in Protestant society? Perhaps the culmination of a long process of cultural disembodiment of women—i.e., the refusal to recognize women as body and language incarnating another vision of life—with its roots in the tenebrous origins of "history." I became once more overwhelmed with the idea that English, that great language of Protestantism, had hidden, under its apparently relatively "fair" surface a sexism greater than any of us expected. (Danish linguist Otto Jespersen, writing in 1905, almost proudly affirms: "... there is one expression that continually comes to my mind whenever I think of the English language and compare it with others: it seems to me positively and expressly *masculine,* it is the language of a grown-up man and has very little childish or feminine about it."[8])

Could women write then, without questioning the language, the very material with which they worked? And since I was a prose writer, what would writing which was also a questioning of language do to the shape of a story or novel? What would it do to the reader who would have to circle back, to become involved in the process of struggling through a text, in order to work her way into this new kind of reading experience?

Which brings me back to the question of "female-sexed" texts ...

French writer Philippe Sollers: *"Je dirai que la reine Victoria, en chemin de fer, en train de lire un roman du XIXe siècle, c'est l'image parfaite du point zéro où peut en arriver la littérature. Il y a là une période d'anesthésie ...'*[9]

Feminist writers everywhere know of the struggle to express a reality that has been mute with a language tailored to the needs of a society where the Phallus is *signifiant*. Although the material arising from the current wave of feminist consciousness very quickly starts hammering away at the boundaries of form, the assumption among most Anglo-American feminists until recently[10] has been that language, syntax, genre are not important enough issues to merit serious debate. Québécois women writers have played a vanguard role in the growing awareness of the relationship between language and struggle for change. But whether there will be, in English Canada, the kind of energetic fusion between feminism, and revolt in language and form, that characterized Québec women's writing of the late 70s remains to be seen. Canada's history is different from Québec's, particularly its history of progressive struggle. In Québec, language has always been a political issue. This was further fueled by the cultural connection with France and the language-focused issues raised by poststructuralists (Roland Barthes, Jacques Derrida) and by feminists like Luce Irigaray and Hélène Cixous. Also, in Québec, since the beginning of the nationalist movement, avant-garde writers have been a point of political/cultural reference, another factor which facilitated the emergence of a deeply contestative group of women writers in this culture.

Still, we've heard a call for female-sexed texts and something deep in us responds—although not without doubts.

Maybe the call does not suit our English-Canadian needs. We have to find our *own* solutions—and debunk our *own* myths. What we can learn, I think, from French-speaking feminist writers is their insistence on asserting *la différence féminine* as context. It's an assertion that rests on the confidence that the feminine exists as something culturally positive, at least potentially. But perhaps the feminine does stand as a dimmer shadow in our English-Protestant heritage. This may be another reason why English-Canadian feminist writing has tended to be content-oriented compared to the more radical contestation of language and form that has taken place in Québec.

And what does all this have to do with the writing of prose? Plenty, I think. I see the leaves rushing along an autumnal St. Denis St. sidewalk. France is waiting for me in a café for what we called one of *nos dimanches durassiens*. The café has a very "contemporary" setting: nostalgic old Québec décor and a heavy drug trade in the washrooms. Our talk is very "modern," too: we talk of *l'écriture*, rarely of the novel or short story, or the poem. A fire crackles in the fireplace. Around us are couples, children, artists. Perhaps I notice especially the women with their bright colours, their well-groomed hair, because in our heads ring the voices, the words of other women writers. This is a period where I'm reading almost nothing but women, mostly in French, and nearly always women who are forerunners of or participants in *la modernité*: Duras, Kristeva, Stein, Wittig, Brossard, Irigaray, Cixous, Emma Santos, Sophie Podolski, (both dead, young, of suicide), Bersianik. All of them confirm what we already feel— that to express the shape of our desire, our prose must lean towards poetry (wise old Virginia had predicted this decades ago), and poetry can no longer look "like a poem" on the page. They also confirm our doubts about sentences and the relationships of verb to subject. We're listening hard to each other and scraps of our conversations end up in each other's writing. This text, for example. Or her novel, *Nous parlerons comme on écrit*.[11] One of the things we have learned in our quest is that, having for so long existed as the fiction of patriarchy, writing our own stories now is often, at least in part, a biographical process. My prose writing becomes part of a spiral-like movement, linked in space and time to the work of other women in Québec and elsewhere. It IS and is more exalted because it's part of a community.

If I quoted modernist French writer Philippe Sollers at the beginning of this section, it was not to deny my respect for Jane Austen, George Eliot, the Brontës. Nor for more contemporary writers like Margaret Laurence. But we are not only women living at the end of the twentieth century, but also women who—thanks to the struggles of the last twenty years—are hearing ourselves better, more profoundly than ever before.

Unfortunately, before being able to publish the new work expressing this subject-in-process, these new sounds, we have to shout down the precedents. I find it fascinating that two of the most "modern" American pre-war women writers, Gertrude Stein and Djuna Barnes, wrote out of Paris. What would have happened to their writing in Milwaukee or even in New York? Indeed, for a contemporary English-language woman writer, dealing with English literature is like dealing with English law. The precedents come back to haunt you. The critics remind you that the English novel in its present form was to a great extent shaped by the writing of women. So what's all the fuss? I have even heard it said that the experimental work of Québec's new women writers has (paradoxically of course) something to do with the Catholic imagination, whereas the English-Canadian (Protestant) imagination is irrevocably realist (read accessible and possibly anti-intellectual) and that's that. No use looking to the left for support either. Because if you fool around with the meat and potatoes of syntax and form, you render the work inaccessible to "ordinary people"—the bulk of whom think, we are led to believe, like white, middle-class males. The same group who brought us television and the newspapers.

Still, the process of knocking the written word into some new shape better suited to our use goes on, it seems, with increasing insistence. A community is being formed, cutting across cultures and resistances. I know my relationship with France and other Québécois women writers opened me early to ideas not easily accessible to most anglophones. (Luce Irigaray, for example, perhaps for women writers one of the most important theoreticians living today, has only recently been translated.[12]) But it also led me to a new vision of my own culture inasmuch as I could study that culture reflected in the eyes of the cultural (and colonized) other. This distanced and lucid bead on patriarchal culture is in fact eventually shared by any group of women working together as a community of writers. For regardless of the language we speak, the culture we live in, we always have the double sense of both belonging and being excluded.

Standing on the outside—the better, perhaps, to create.

Montréal, 1981

NOTES

1 Colette, *Earthly Paradise* (selected extracts), ed. Robert Phelps, (Harmondsworth: Penguin, 1974), p. 191.

2 Luce Irigaray, *Ce Sexe qui n'en est pas un* (Paris: Les Editions de Minuit, 1977), p. 37.

3 Colette, p. 132.

4 Claude Beausoleil, unedited text, March, 1981.

5 Nicole Brossard, *Le Centre blanc* (Montréal: Les Editions d'Orphée, 1970). My reading here of this piece is coloured by readings of later Brossard

work. It was in about 1973 that Brossard started insisting on the specifically feminine in the act of writing.

6 Hélène Cixous, "The Laugh of the Medusa," trans. Keith Cohen and Paula Cohen, *New French Feminisms,* ed. Elaine Marks and Isabelle de Courtivron (New York: Schocken, 1981), p. 251.

7 Michel Tremblay, *Thérèse et Pierrette à l'ecole des Saints-Anges* (Montréal: Léméac, 1980).

8 Author's insertion, added 1988. Jesperson's *Growth and Structure of the English Language* (Chicago University Press, 1982) can be read as the historical account of the growing sharpening and efficacy of English, at the expense, in part, of the feminine, until grammar, lexicon and *"words and turns that are found, and words and turns that are not found"* combine to give English its masculine clarity.

9 Philippe Sollers, *Vision à New York* (Paris: Grasset, 1981), p. 155.

10 There were of course brave forerunners who raised these issues in their writing, from Virginia Woolf to Mary Daly. But the first time I heard language, syntax, grammar discussed collectively in English as a feminist issue was at the Women and Words conference in Vancouver in 1983.

11 France Théoret, *Nous parlerons comme on écrit* (Montréal: Les Herbes Rouges, 1982).

12 Author's insertion, added 1988: *Speculum of the Other Woman,* trans. Gillian C. Gill, and *This Sex Which Isn't One,* trans. Catherine Porter, are now available in English (Ithaca: Cornell University Press, 1985).

A VISIT TO CANADA

The question of self and other, of differences and likenesses among women, indeed, the very meaning of the word "sisterhood," has become broader, more complex, in this decade. For one thing, the assumption that all women stand in the same relationship to patriarchy has been substantially nuanced. Among writers, this acknowledgement of difference has contributed to a cross-fertilization of ideas and mutual respect between feminists from Québec and Canada that is quite unusual in the pan-Canadian context.

Still, the question begs: how much space really exists for the differences of women of other races and cultures? Traveling in English Canada, I sometimes sense an imputation of exoticism to Québécois women which leaves me feeling that, under the surface of our raised consciousnesses are buried less positive latent attitudes, vestiges of the conquest mentality of our history. Even as an English Quebecer who has absorbed considerable influences from a French-language culture not the Same as the dominant English culture of other provinces, I have occasionally felt a small personal malaise regarding this lack of space in Canada for the hearing of difference. Small, at least, compared to the malaise caused by our white failure to hear women of colour and women from developing countries. But the experience has been part of my learning how not hearing the other closes space for each of us (both the speaker and the addressee). Our feminist striving for pluralism—growing out of our collective insistence on our validation as women in the context of patriarchy—is one of the most progressive aspects of feminist discourse. To succeed in applying this pluralism to everyday life would have remarkable consequences for our writing....

IN A CAFE ON The Main, poet Erin Mouré is reading me an Olga Broumas translation of an Odysseas Elytis poem. The poem is a list of nouns, sensual words from the Greek poet's place of dwelling that wash over me in a wave of pleasure ... *cistern, citrus, Claire, clear sailing, cliffs, clockwork, coloured pebbles, cool wind,* etc. Words of a Greek male poet translated by a Greek-American lesbian, translated again into sound by the voice of Erin, who grew up in Alberta, reading to me, an English Quebecer, in a dark Montréal café, at a long string of tables reaching from mirrors at one end to the street at the other. The words revealing the possible richness in the reading / writing relationship of a work that crosses cultures, sexual boundaries, or that is merely transmitted from one individual to another, each reading affected by the reader's sense of place, her sexuality, among other things.

Also, doubtless, in such transmissions, there is terrible loss. Particularly when the reader / writer stand in a conflictual relationship to each other. In Canada, for example, the strikingly different Québécois and Canadian perceptions (readings) of the October Crisis are part of two ongoing different narratives in what is officially a common history. What visceral sources these different narratives seem to have, springing from a deeply emotional place where our personal, social, political cultures meet! Clearly, they are more than content, are a question of texture. Even an anglophone living in Québec, provided she lives a good part of the time in French, starts to feel this difference in her body after awhile.

At least, she starts to feel it on visits to the other culture: English-Canada. This overly-acute awareness of self may be the self-consciousness of a woman socialized to attend to the reactions of others. At any rate, when I travel west from Montréal I always feel dressed "funny." My haircuts too extreme, my clothes too crazy, my shoes too fancy. The discipline, the eye for detail in clothes which I have absorbed from

my milieu, seems in contradiction with what people, particularly in progressive milieus farther west, seem to like. Dressing
well in English somehow implies not drawing too much attention towards oneself. So that when my brother, who lives with
his five children in Victoria—in a sprawling stuccoed house
complete with garden, weaving loom, and the smell of home-
made bread in the kitchen—introduces me to his youngest
daughter, she says: "You're joking, Daddy. That's not your sister." And I feel, sitting on his sofa in my black pointed boots,
my black-and-white striped sweater, my trendy pants cut wide
at the hips and narrow at the ankles, like a misplaced dandy.
The problem being that the (bilingual) body knows both
dress codes intimately, is aware of how each culture reads
them, the beauty in them, and also what disturbs the eye of
the beholder. So that they join, almost comically, like the
clashing signs of a Popova painting, somewhere in a core
image of "self."

This internal clashing of the relatively superficial dress
codes from two distinct cultures is only one sign of the internal confusion that can arise from a sense of "difference." It
explains in part the temptation to play the role of *bridge* on
more significant fronts as the body moves from one culture to
another. On visits to Canada, I am frequently reminded that
my relationship to English, my mother culture, is also traves-
tied in two directions in my writing, my discourse. Sometimes,
when on tour giving public readings, I'm almost relieved that
the weight of Anglo-Saxon narrative traditions remains as a
kind of superego over my shoulder. So that I might provide
the audience with some semblance of the story (I think) they
want. On the other hand, the French in my ear, a French
coloured by the politics and struggles of *les Québécois(es)*
over two decades, has altered my English "line" of thinking,
and in the process somewhat collapsed other genres into my
prose. While it's true that I have not experienced the *text,* that
distillation of fiction and theory, as intensely as my Québécois

colleagues, the endless translation of ideas in my writing from French to English, in my speech from English to French, often forces the confrontation of reflexive and imaginary writing in the same text. The cultural doubleness making that self-reflexiveness necessary in order not to drown in confusion, much like the doubleness women experience vis-à-vis male-dominant culture.

It was precisely in order to explore that gap between male-dominant culture and an emerging culture in-the-feminine, that feminists writing in Québec created, in the 70s, a new genre: *fiction-theory*. This was not *theory about fiction,* but rather . . . a reflexive doubling-back over the texture of the text. Where nothing, not even the "theory" escapes the poetry, the internal rhythm (as opposed to the internal logic) of the writing. The better to break continuity (the continuity of patriarchal mythologies) into fragments in order to question syntax / context. This habit of stopping to reflect on the process within the text itself looks forward toward a meaning in-the-feminine. Mutable meaning, open-ended, signified by the way Nicole Brossard uses the hologram—for a utopian reflection of woman into the future—at the end of her novel, *picture theory* (1982).

And fiction-theory, while it may be a method of exploring a space, a gap (never pretending to close it) between two or more ways of thinking, is the antithesis of a *bridge*. What the expression has meant to us writing in Québec is that a woman might express her own unique difference. The lucidity of the theoretical process—in itself an intertextual process involving reading, talking, in which the words of other women play a key role—constantly prepares the way for the new risks she herself moves towards in her own fiction. At first (late 70s, early 80s), I felt, on visits to Canada, that these new ideas from Québec were received with reticence. This I attributed to a "populist" bias of progressive political culture in English-Canada—a bias implying, among other things, a single notion of accessibility. The perception proved to be, in part, ill-founded. For among women, there were many concerned with the relationship between feminism and language. I began getting invited to speak in Canada about this issue from a Québec perspective. Somehow, in the process, I fell into the role of bridge, a bridge from French Québec to, say, English Vancouver, or Toronto, or Windsor. A bridge that went right over myself, casting a shadow that left little trace of either my writing or my reflection on it. It is a mistake we women often make: the habit of obliterating the self in the name of some ill-defined patriarchal rigour. Or just to please others. And it raises the question of how for whom we write (imagine we write) or speak alters what we write or speak. What is called in French *le rapport d'adresse*.

In the function of bridge or go-between, there is no equitable give-and-take. It is a function where the body of the speaker is what is lost in the interests of objective pedagogy. I felt crabby playing this role, unsure whether I was laying it on myself, or whether the growing adoration of Québec by certain anglo intellectuals (a too abrupt turn-around of the biases that had existed before?) just meant that the messenger had been forgotten in the process. I did sense that people in English Canada often thought of me as having precisely the same culture as themselves. Their not sensing my difference, my efforts at translating *within* my own language to make my words, in part borrowed from another culture, understandable, "accessible" to them even as I spoke, was frustrating. More importantly, I think, it reflects the arrogant assumptions of any dominant culture: i.e., that a minority culture (Québec) does not have the vitality to operate as a sphere of influence on those "minorities" (anglophones) that live within its parameters.

The plane to Vancouver landed in the fog, as it always seems to. In my briefcase a paper titled "Body / Language / Text." It started by making a point about the relationship between body, text and writing with a reference to the French writer Roland Barthes.

... Summing up his likes and dislikes, Barthes says he likes *salad, cinammon, cheese, marzipan,* etc. He doesn't like *white pomeranians, women in slacks (sic), geraniums, strawberries, the harpsichord,* etc. All this proves, he concludes, is that his body is different from anyone else's....[1]

No doubt using Barthes was my way of justifying what I feared might be regarded as "essentialist" by male (post)modernists in the audience. That is, my sense that the writing subject is not neutral, that gender coding cannot be absent from the text.[2] That if small things like tastes in food could be considered part of a larger inscription signifying a body's distinctiveness, so then also must one's pen be influenced, in its inscribing, by one's (often unconscious?) perception (reading) of the gendered body guiding that pen.

The point about how gender might affect one's relationship to language was best underscored by using Irigaray's radical and poignant way of asserting the connection between a woman speaking (as opposed to being spoken in the patriarchal mirror) and the movements, rhythms of her body, particuarly her sexuality[3] (as opposed to fucking, to put it bluntly, as t(he)y expect(s)). I am aware of the dangers of speculating as regards the impact of gender on speech or writing. For it is difficult to separate the effect of one's biology (*and* one's sexual orientation) on one's relationship to language from the impact of other types of social conditioning, such as race and class. Yet to suppress the awareness of sexual difference, if one speaks from a minority position, is to risk the drowning of that difference in the expectations of the dominant other.

But, who really expects what of the body of the other? How do I, the speaking subject, respond to what I think that expectation is? On that trip to Vancouver, my decision to play a certain role meant that only part of my narrative could be transmitted. The irony was that the texts of the Québécois women about whom I was talking had somehow been involved in a weaving, had been intertexts to my own work in the previous five years. So that dwelling on Nicole Brossard's version of fiction-theory, for example, was saying implicitly what I couldn't say outright. What I had buried in the interests of being the "Québec expert." MYSELF.

"The private is political, I improvise on new ground. I take back my rights, what is due me.... Words surface, coming from afar.... I exhibit me for us, that which resembles us. I write and I don't want to do it alone ..."[4]

Also, in speaking of Louky Bersianik's relentless efforts to get beyond syntax's refusal of the female subject, I was speaking of a collective project. *"Something hasn't happened that should have happened. The image-attic has been pillaged, havoc has been wreaked in the memory box. All that's left is the somebody saids; the what-would-they-says; all that's left is the water sprites, the shock waves of the shimmering ripples of a single facet of memory, its ticklish unglorious part. All that remains, monstrously, is women's amnesia." "Will we or will we not,"* continues Louky in her wonderful text, *Les Agénisées du vieux monde,*[5] *"enumerate and analyze all existence to try and separate out that which belongs to us, to rediscover ourselves?"*

The temptation of the bridge is to substitute what others want for that impossible, contradictory grasping towards "selfhood." As I see it, "selfhood" for women is not being *one* (the unary subject male modernists have been "deconstructing"). It is not being an essential core or a singular definition; it is process and it is plural. The self-reflexiveness of fiction-theory would not have its politically progressive implications if it did not depend on an intertextual play with the works of other women. Significantly, after my talk in Vancouver, where I quoted Roland Barthes, Nicole Brossard, Louky Bersianik, etc., a woman in the audience said: "Very interesting, but I would have liked to hear more about you."

She was right: what can women offer a new civilization if it is not the deep acceptance of difference (and *différance*)[6] within the collective? However small my differences are as an anglo-Québécoise vis-à-vis the dominant culture in the pan-Canadian context (and however great they are as a rebellious woman in patriarchy), asserting them is offering yet one more challenge to the bland assumption of sameness (i.e., one is (thinks) the same as the dominant other) which is the hall-mark of patriarchy and dominant cultures everywhere. In this feminist way of thinking lies a potentially profound under-standing of the relationship between art, politics, culture, more subtle, complex, than populist notions of accessibility and socialist-realist ideas about representation. At its heart is the ever mutable *rapport d'adresse* between the artist as speaking body and those (the first circle) whom she chooses to address. Altering, as I have said, not only the work but also the addresser and the addressee.

The best illustration I can think of is how my writing is altered if I direct it towards women, towards my female writ-ing peers, as opposed to my male peers. Each direction brings out something different in my work. But in terms of the collec-tive task implied by the expression "feminist writing" over the past decade, the line we trace between the space we write from and those we write towards, has taken on a special meaning. I remember turning round and round a text, unable to write it as long as I imagined my reader as a male critic or even a male editor. It was only when I had established an imaginary *rapport d'adresse* with certain women readers that the text could come into being. As if the essence of my think-ing process at that moment, hence of language, could not be touched as long as my movement through the text also involved an act of translation for the purpose of communicat-ing with the male other, particularly if he were in a position of power concerning my writing.

But which women readers? This rapport or relationship

between writer and reader, or between writer and writer (both the intellect and the body are implied in the French word *adresse*), is a performance that reaches out to a select and immediate audience. A performance that requires a response, so that a dialogic process is set up—a process which by no means excludes the male reader, but which, for women to actually finally occupy space within culture, must first take place—at a certain level—among ourselves. How else to avoid the painful loss I spoke of earlier which is inevitable in translation?

And what if I had sought, on that trip to Vancouver, to establish a veritable *rapport d'adresse* (a give-and-take dialogue) with certain women in the audience, by assuming my own text, rather than suppressing it? Was there anything in their experience that would have prepared them to hear my difference? What sort of *rapport d'adresse* between writer and reader is possible when a text is nourished by and written in one cultural context, and published and read in another? When, as is my case, the nourishing of the text happens in French, a language present but not necessarily directly represented in the writing, the speaking, the reading of the text, which all happen in English. My texts leave Québec, where they are read in (French) translation by my Québécois peers, to "visit" Canada where they are read in English. And these Canadian readers, without thinking, because they live in the house of their language, expect my work to have a direct - *rapport* with the concerns raised in their English community. Assume—unless they're "used to me"—things of it which they do not expect of a translation from French. For example, that it be coloured more by readings of the narratives of an Alice Munro, a Margaret Laurence, even an Audrey Thomas, than by the experimental forms of a Louky Bersianik or a Nicole Brossard.

This gap between the culture of the reading community and that of the community from which the text is written probably affects the text even on the level of syntax. For the writer is constantly taking wild leaps over those cultural gaps, translating in two directions, an exercise both fascinating and terrifying in its implications (notably, the fear of failing to "communicate"). Until she realizes that she has no choice but to try, in her writing process, to leave spaces into which the other, the reader, can read her own difference. So that each difference may be confronted, felt within the text.

But this is very idealistic. For everywhere are patterns of dominance, assumptions of sameness to be challenged. A text, for example, carrying an unacknowledged cultural difference in the country called Canada can't help but implicitly challenge certain assumptions about language (and about Canadian history) held by most anglophones, whose relationship to language is not, historically, one of oppression.

There are other paradoxes in the reception of a work, too. What is the effect on a work, for example, when a critical reading in the receiving community is qualitatively positive but is also *slant*, to use an Emily Dickinson expression? That is, the critical text "loses" much of the fictional text, due to the critic's distance from the preoccupations of the cultural community in which the fictional text was produced. Sometimes when I read criticism of my work coming from English Canada, I have to translate the criticism. By that I mean I have to guess where the critic is writing from, guess at its subtext coming from its community fabric, in order to understand it. How much more frustrating and irksome must this situation be for women whose cultures are non-European?

Yet, for my part, these "visits" to Canada, sometimes complex and painful, have also been, increasingly, hopeful. The awareness of, the space for language and cultural differences (and likenesses) between Québécois women and anglo-Canadian women has opened considerably in the last five years. Are we white feminists capable of leaving open, in our hearing of racial, ethnic, regional differences, the space for the integral other that we have claimed for ourselves in our discourse on, among others, *new writing in-the-feminine?* It seems to me that the cultural leaps we women make through the spaces of bias and prejudice in our own culture must be synchronic with the fact that we can no longer pretend any language, any culture, has fixed meaning and values. In this, hopefully, we have gained some understanding and solidarity, despite our differences, vis-à-vis patriarchal culture. The more we grasp that in a sense all of us have a double, perhaps multiple relationship towards the culture that surrounds us, the more we will be able to acknowledge differences, oppressions, hierarchies, among women. And the more we will be able to stop some of the loss of translation.

Sitting in that café on The Main listening to the voice of a poet, a lesbian, reading me a poet from another country, another alphabet, whom she loves, translated by yet another poet, Olga Broumas, Greek as the poet Odysseas Elytis is Greek, yet, also, a woman like us, I think: this is a safe translation. Somehow, here, has been established a string of equalities that transforms possible loss (there is always inevitably loss) into wealth. The energies—the cultures bouncing off one another in the café whose tables are lined up like a string of images—headed towards the energy of the street.

Montréal, 1986, 1988

NOTES

1   Roland Barthes, *Roland Barthes by Roland Barthes,* trans. Richard Howard (New York: Hill & Wang, 1977).

2   Both French- and English-language feminists interested in post-structuralism have held that language practice is sexually coded by the "user." (*The use of all language by the dominant-male has led to the sexualization of language, and woman finds herself facing an excision of the real,* wrote Québécois writer Louise Dupré, trans. Daphne Marlatt and

Kathy Mezei, in *Room of One's Own,* Vol. 8, No. 4, Vancouver, 1984.) However, there is also a current of North American followers of the French poststructuralist Jacques Derrida who consider the feminist position "essentialist," i.e., that it biologically overdetermines one's relationship to language. It amuses me that proponents of Derridean *différance* cannot see the wide range of different positions on this subject within the feminist community, where the discussion is far from over.

See, also, Lola Lemire Tostevin's wonderful treatment of this debate in her text on attending a class taught by Derrida in *'sophie* (Toronto: Coach House Press, 1988), pp. 45-48.

3 Luce Irigaray, notably in *Ce Sexe qui n'en est pas un* (Paris: Les Editions de Minuit, 1977).

4 Nicole Brossard, "L'Ecrivain," *La Nef des sorcières* (Montréal: Les Editions Quinze, 1976), pp. 74-75 (trans. Gail Scott).

5 Louky Bersianik, *Les Agénisées du vieux monde* (Montréal: L'Intégrale Editrice, 1982), p. 5, p. 12 (trans. Gail Scott).

6 *Différance* is a Derridean term, combining both the idea of inscription of *difference* and *of the deferment of meaning* (fr. *différer*) in writing-as-textual-practice. Its pluralist connotations make it an important concept for feminists who have often applied it to writing in-the-feminine without necessarily naming it as such.

2

ABOUT FORM

A Story Between
Two Chairs

Devenir écrivain, c'est oublier qu'avant tout on est écrivant, qu'on a un rapport de travail avec le texte. Il y a le travail transformateur du texte et la matière transformée, c'est le corps de l'écrivant. On a trop conformé la modernité à des paramètres objectifs. La modernité ça ne se passe pas seulement sur une page: c'est un rapport à l'écriture et à la vie."

Normand de Bellefeuille, in "Vouloir la fiction,"
la nouvelle barre du jour, 1984

The astonishing influence feminist writers have had on contemporary writing in Québec is reflected in this passage. Normand de Bellefeuille, a key figure of Québécois modernity, speaks of writing here in terms of the relationship between writing, body, life, much as feminist writers did at a 1984 colloquium in Montréal "Vouloir la fiction." *Organized by the periodical* la nouvelle barre du jour, *the colloquium was essentially a discussion on the fate of* la modernité *in the reactionary 80s. There was some tension between feminists and their supporters, on one hand, and a small group of writers who said they were fed up with modernist "inhibitions" (read, among other things, political consciousness: for the self-reflexive aspect of modernity in Québec has generally assumed the writer to be in an oppositional stance to dominant ideology). The tension itself was a sign of the impact of feminism on contemporary writing in Québec in the decade 1975-85.*

The "fiction" wished for or desired in the naming of this colloquium was the fiction of the text, with its "theoretical imagination," with its refusal of genres, notably of the separation of fiction and theory. And, yes, the text had been greatly shaped in Québec by women writers. But it WAS 1984, and the literary avant garde was suffering from the same temptation as the political avant garde a few years earlier: the temptation to step out, however briefly, from what sometimes seemed like an overly ascetic marginality. Some of us had novels in our drawers. Essays were being considered.... Was the text about to be swallowed by a new reformism?

Fiction 1984. A woman sitting in the corridor. Trying to avoid the clichés. Does *fiction* mean "une création de l'imagination" (Larousse) or is it "fictitious literature, esp. the novel or short story" (Webster)?
I know. Compromise. Adopt the hybrid. How feminine! Yes, weave the open into narrative. The story as pretext. Practice is an ambiguous space between cultures. Fiction: A woman sitting in the corridor. Outside the sounds of war. Cacophony of clichés. She writes. Listening to the animal inside her. Trying to fix a line between music (women's voices) and God the Father. But in which cultural code? Hi-tech, anti-nuclear, revolution . . . feminism. No discourse is pure. Just women sitting in the corridor. Looking at all the world a stage of men. She writes in another language (not French). Doubly distanced from her sisters. Your own fault if English in Québec. So stay guilty: an inverted reflection can give an extremely theatrical perception. Self as irony. Unaffirmable. Not serious. Thus in contradiction with feminism. Pale amazon perversely drawn by the complexity of "tragedy." She writes. Who for? From the tunnel to Dora's fortress. Outside the sounds of war. She writes. The better to see herself. Identity needs appearances. Storybook surfaces. So tell a story. Narrate a little order in the decadence. The holes show. Never mind. Under the surface the fragments. But who can speak of that? The family's back ...

Montréal, 1984

61

A part of the colloquium proceedings was published in la
nouvelle barre du jour *alongside our texts....*
"What do you mean by listening to the animal inside her?"
*(one of the writers asked). I had to admit I meant listening to
something* essentially *"feminine,"—perhaps to a part of "self"
(i.e. self-as-woman) not quite integrated into the law, closer to
"nature." In modernist terms this was heresy. But, hidden
behind that* animal inside her *(I imagined it as a tiger painted
on a screen), lay the real difference between feminist writing
practice and that of non-feminists identifying with modernity.
A question of process ... For the modernist desire to disperse the
writing "I" across an experimental space (i.e., to deconstruct
traditional hierarchies of author / text / reader) unfortunately
too often gets articulated as if every text were written from the
same "universal" locus (male, white, educated). Whereas
feminists interested in modernity see the problem differently.
Among others, the universality of the writing subject (and the
degree of its author-ity in relationship to the writing) cannot be
assumed—since many women have a sense of being already
fragmented, alienated by male fictions. MY desire was to create
a new female subject-in-process through the act of writing—
which act was also a process of deconstructing traditional
fictions about women. I knew the "animal inside me" was a
reflection of something else, a wish, a dream. But could a
woman write without this dream, this imagining of a no longer
muted feminine?*
*On the other hand, I was also starting to feel uncomfortable
with the restrictive way "feminism" sometimes gets applied to
writing practice: the rigid attitudes prevailing in certain
milieus about what a "feminist heroine" is, for example, have
progressed little beyond the social realism of the 20s and 30s. If
writing is the act of always seeking more understanding, more
lucidity, prescriptive directives have no place in our trajectory
towards the uncanny edge of language. I said, in answer to a
question on that issue,* "Feminism is a way of life for me. But

when I write I feel I can be confident my feminism is a given without having to check constantly if my text is "correct." ... *In other words, I trust that my political consciousness is part and parcel of my personal integrity, hence of my way of thinking. But, I will not let it play the role of superego.*

I was also asked what I meant by "pale amazon, perversely attracted by the fascination of 'tragedy.'" My reply: To be anglophone in Québec is to shoulder a history which renders one guilty, which diminishes the self-image of the politically sensitive person, at least as far as her relationship to history is concerned. *When you find yourself in this historical conundrum, and at the same time you feel a tremendous solidarity with what has been going on in the way of (Québécois) national affirmation in the past twenty years, the positive, upbeat image often expected of feminist fiction seems oversimplified.* It's one of the reasons why I'm often tempted in my writing to inverse things, usually ironically, to the dark side of the paradigm.

SHAPING A VEHICLE
FOR HER USE

As I've said, a woman, when she writes about writing, seems to require more than the purely discursive. Julia Kristeva, for example, invokes a "post-Freudian rationality"—two stages or levels of text to take into account the conscious and the unconscious—to write her essays. This requirement is not a pose, but an imposition, which, I think, has to do with the link of the unconscious in women's writing to the repressed (female) body. It indicates, therefore, a necessary disturbance of the rational surface of what is usually considered a "theoretical" text.

My writing about writing frequently happens in the spaces between my fictional output, the theoretical observations coming after the risk of writing is taken. Yet, they spur on the next act of fiction. In fact, the fictional "risk" depends, to some extent, on the capacity of the theoretical imagination to leap forward even as it sums up what went before. But the process is not chronological: the fiction often interrupts the theoretical imagination as if, when writing about writing, I too cannot forget the body through which the words proceed.

The body's possible imprint on form is particularly underscored in this text, perhaps because it was originally prepared for the landmark Women and Words Conference (Vancouver, 1983).

WE WOMEN HAVE two ways of speaking. The first begins in our mother's womb as we listen to the rhythms of her body (likewise for our brothers). As girls, we continue to develop this largely oral tongue in our ongoing relationship and identification with her (here, said Freud, our brothers start to differ). But at the same time we are developing another relationship to the "fathertongue" of education, the media, the law—all patriarchal institutions. Consequently, we end up with a split relationship to language: there is the undernurtured woman's voice, badly heard outside in what my mother always called a "man's world," and the other language, the one we try to speak in order to bridge the gap.

But what form, story, if the girl child's progress into culture is the very source of her fractured identity? Freud called it the Oedipus complex—that threshold of language / identity over which the little girl scurries back and forth, while the boy steps securely into the father's realm. We women are often painfully aware of the consequent doubleness of our speech: when speaking publicly to mixed groups, for instance, or ... when writing. "It takes a lot of energy to be inhabited by a man who thinks like a man in the world of men and a woman who insists on remaining true to her womanhood," says French writer Claudine Herrmann.[1]

Yes, what form, story, if writing for women is a bridge between different ways of speaking?

Or, is this the wrong way to pose the question?

I'm not sure if I "rationally" came to the conclusion to temporarily forget story (i.e. plot, character, form). The better to let language take the lead in making "sense" of the socially fragmented female "core" *(corps)*; to transform how I wrote, thought, the better to transform my life. But slowly I learned (writing and erasing) that I had to risk subverting the story form, in order to write stories "shaped" like me. This resulted in certain English-speaking male writers and editors saying "nothing happened" in my stories. The build-up, the dramatic climax (that old saw), they said, was fuzzed or missing. "There are too many distractions from the dramatic throughline," one fiction magazine editor wrote me. "What does the narrator want?" (Remember when people used to ask: What does Québec want?) "What will she do to get it? What is stopping her?" I thought: he doesn't understand the influence of Québécois literature on English writing in Québec. I showed my work to a well-known Montréal English playwright. He said: "I like your early stories. Now you're trying to be too academic. Just a whole lot of images going nowhere."

But, there is nothing academic about trying to reproduce the rhythm of women's speech patterns. About *listening*, hence trying to express what surges from "inside" (that buried subtext of mothertongue?) but has been traditionally reduced to silence. Of course, this emphasis on listening, on writing what she *hears*, may require plot to take a second seat to voice. Even if story, given its tradition of being told, could be viable in some form, since it seems able to approximate the written and oral word. We just have to discard this insistence that the story "make something happen," that it have action, something dramatic (like a war or political coup?), as irrelevant to a woman's way of seeing. In *La Violence du calme*, French writer Viviane Forrester situates the beginning of patriarchy at the moment when God, in collusion with the devil, got Adam and Eve to "sin," thus interrupting their happy idyl on the grass. An event had to take place on which a drama could be based, on which power could be modeled, she says.[2]

Still, I call my writing "stories,"—as if it were easier to modify a genre than find a new one. Perhaps I can't altogether abandon narrative: it makes me feel secure. But my "stories" lean towards text, are a hybrid—like *Pure and The Impure,* my favorite book by Colette. I love this collection of short works for how it oddly combines story, social criticism on subjects like Don Juanism, and autobiography. Women's fiction is often highly autobiographical. Why not? When what is called "real" (the female figure in *their* stories, in *their* legal, educational and other institutions) seems like fiction to us. It's interesting that the closer women get to naming this "real" on our own terms, the more uncomfortable men get. That's why men were so angry at not being able to attend the Women & Words conference. That's why Colette's second husband was bitterly critical of the autobiographical tendencies and the alleged obsession with sex in her work.

Fortunately, this hasn't stopped women from ignoring the boundaries of genre since long before "modernity." Virginia Woolf's novels often comprise shorter pieces surfacing like fragments of a poetic mosaic (*The Waves*), or shot through with drama, essay (*Between The Acts*). Even if we take the short story in the strictest sense, we find outstanding women writers have subverted the genre even as they asserted new women's voices. Gertrude Stein, Jane Bowles, Anaïs Nin (in among other things, the fragments of her diary), more recently Marguerite Duras, whose novels have grown shorter and shorter, more and more poetic. And in Canada, Sheila Watson. What links these women is their excesses, the crazy way they took risks in their writing. Stein and her sentences. Bowles' characters, leaning wildly over the edge of hysteria. Nin's fictional promiscuity. Watson's theoretical sophistication. Paradoxically, these excesses are problematic for certain approaches to feminist criticism (Bowles' *lack of* "strong women," Stein's *lack of* accessibility, Nin's *overwrought* heterosexuality, etc.). Indeed, a content-focused "feminist" analysis of such texts might even bring forth the kind of reproaches we often get from men: the accusation of being either not enough, or else too much....

But since we're talking *story,* perhaps we should, at least, define the parameters of discussion. How does a woman choose a form to write in? Is there a connection between the form she chooses and the circumstances of her life? Writing at the turn of the century, Virginia Woolf insisted in both *A Room of One's Own* and *Three Guineas* that, to write, a woman must have an economic situation permitting her to concentrate in peace and quiet. So, in answer to the question, is the story really to be privileged over longer fiction, the materialist in me is tempted to reply: a woman's socioeconomic situation may be a determining factor. Maybe she has a job; maybe she has children. In terms of time, a woman's life is never simple; she must put aside her writing to do a million other things. To make matters worse, her socialization has trained her to keep her mind so cluttered with details that concentration on a longer work is often, at least initially, difficult....

Except, I know that form, the form we choose, inevitably represents a deeply felt necessity of which the material prerogative is only a small part. Virginia Woolf also understood this, already, at the beginning of the century. "The novel alone," she wrote, "was young enough to be soft in her hands (that is, in the hands of the great nineteenth-century women novelists). Yet who shall say that even now 'the novel' is rightly shaped for her use? No doubt we shall find her ... providing some new vehicle, not necessarily in verse, for the poetry in her."[3] Which brings me to another point about the story: never a highly marketable form of writing, it remains a literary genre for which the established conventions are relatively few. What I like about this relative lack of precedent is that it tends to confuse the little censor lurking within all of us, the little man who represents literary norms and criteria, thus giving us space to play with new rhythms and concepts of time and space. The short story, says Julio Cortazar, is shaped like a sphere.[4] A sphere: a nice feminine shape to take off from, a shape that gives us the latitude to avoid linear time, that cause-and-effect time of patriarchal logic. Yes, the sphere is precisely the kind of shape, of movement, that permits us to leave reasonable prose behind. It's a shape that abets (my) departure from a horizontal plane of writing, the better to decipher a memory blocked by silence, to leap from my discoveries towards a future not yet dreamed of. Twisting, altering in the process, the sphere itself, not to mention the use of certain words, and, inevitably, of syntax. Marguerite Duras—who says her novels have become so short, she hesitates to call them novels—writes: "The words come to me, often without articles (so important in French). Grammatical time follows at a distance."[5] The novel, as Woolf also foresaw, distracts us from this process, or makes it difficult with its demand for a forward thrust, for a plot the reader can hold onto for its longer stretch.

The form we choose to use (and to subvert) is also influenced by what motivates us to take up writing in the first place. Among other things, in this era, our alienation, our anger at being "written" (defined) by others. A situation where we have often ended up (and still do) as cultural clichés (notably as either the mother figure, or the prostitute / lover). I, for one, also want to learn what I can from writing (exploring language) about why we have tolerated this ongoing slap in the face for so long. Luce Irigaray offers a suggestion in her critical rereadings of Freud. For the little girl, at the moment of her Oedipal crisis (her movement into culture), the traumatic event that permits her endurance of ongoing degradation is the repression of her libido, leading to the quelling of female aggressive instincts. Henceforth, in order to achieve her femininity, she will have to work much harder than her brother at repressing her impulses—*notably* through the transformation of her sexual activeness into its opposite: passivity. Belgian writer Claire Lejeune explains how devastating the effect of this is on her relationship to language and consequently on female identity:

The girl child is fatally deprived of her chance to master the word of the father because she can't identify with phallic semantics. In order to integrate into traditional social structures she is therefore required to speak a borrowed language.

*Our western educational system has made certain women vir-
tuosos in this borrowed language, by obliterating from early
childhood the countercultural characteristics proper to her
sex.... Women's language can only emerge unfettered outside
the walls of culture.*[6]

But, I don't want to be "outside the walls of culture": I want
to write a story. Perhaps, the story form permits me to be both
relatively unfettered in my use of language, yet not lose my
link with culture. Perhaps "story" is the pretext, the umbilical
cord attaching me (even precariously) to "reality" as I set out
in search of my desire (voice, language?). Hélène Cixous says:
"Woman must write herself; must write about women and
bring women to writing, from which they have been driven
away as violently as from their bodies—for the same reasons,
by the same law, with the same fatal goal. Woman must put
herself into the text—as into history—by her own movement."[7] Yes, this is the way to approach a story: to write listening with all one's woman's pores to the poetry lying just under
the back-fence gossip, the children's bedtime story, the street
outside the window, the voices in the car—not stopping there
but spinning out, all lights blinking, in search of something ...
lost?

But what will this do to plot? Does Cortazar's sphere shape
require a "climax," a rise, a fall? Can it be summed up symbol-
ically by the oneness of the phallic form? And here we are
again at the question of how to get to the shape of our desire
(not the single orgasm of male desire, but the continuous
movement of pleasure of the female sex with its ever-
touching lips)?[8] How, through the deciphering of language in
our writing, to get a sense of the historically absent female
subject? To find a form (a context) in which to recreate her?

In Cortazar's sphere, if it's not rigidly applied (if it's as soft,
as moving, as those female lips), I see after all a starting point,
from which to move towards expressing that voice that has
been a gap in culture. Yet this shape, to permit a circular

exploration, also, to my mind, requires a centre, moving, vortex-like. (*The story as ellipsis—with heart*.) How then to get below the white spaces of the surface, to strip off layers as we move towards expressing the deepest complexities of our emerging culture in-the-feminine? No doubt each writer finds her own devices. Some play with words, using etymology; some bounce off the flat surface of patriarchal ways-of-speaking towards a deeper place.

My awareness of the flat linear surface of reasonable writing came from doing journalism. To get away from it, to break it down in fiction, I first turned towards surrealism, and particularly to that exercise aimed at lifting inhibitions called automatic writing. The focus was partly on the writing down and analysis of dreams through a process of automatic word association. I remember a summer when my entire life seemed to happen at night in my dreams, when days seemed dull and I was reluctant to awake in the morning after the richness of my "night life." A moment close to a kind of madness not in the least frightening. For it was charged with a delicious sense of operating on the limits of language. The more one transgresses, the more one distances from law and order (and what better place to witness this struggle of trying to escape the censor, than in dream work?). Duras says children under five and women who transgress are mad.[9]

But I had to weave all that raw material into form. Finally, I found a way. Inspired by the structures of manifest content in dreams, I wrote stories that were mocking convex surfaces of what I perceived the "real" to be. The spaces left by the spareness of the writing pointing, perhaps, to the gaps in culture where the feminine should be. While the spaces between the fragments that comprised the text emphasized the presence of voice where there had been woman's silence in the past. And I called them "story," regardless of their length; for, again like dreams, which sometimes go on for months, spaced by the wakefulness of the day, the fragments of a story might continue almost infinitely. Which makes me think again, the boundaries of genre are only there to step over.

Yet there is something special about the story. Is it the story's archaic links with forms antecedent to capitalist-patriarchy? Example, the Haitian women's tales, inspired by voodoo—operating as they do on the magic edge of thought. For you can write a story almost as you'd record a dream. First the manifest content: *a woman has left her children in a trailer and is hitchhiking across the prairie*. Then you start playing with the language, with key words on the surface. Towards what latent content will they lead you? When you think you know what the story's (almost) about it's probably finished. This you tell as much by hearing (i.e., feeling happy with the rhythm) as by seeing (grasping meaning).

Historically, women have been validated for their silence. (An old woman I know says her sons "tease" her by threatening to buy a zipper for her lips. Another woman remembers that her father would say "Shut up little Moms" when her mother tried to speak at dinner.) That is, women's *apparent* silence: for between the lines we've been listening to each other. "Nearly the entire history of writing is confounded with the history of reason, of which it is at once the effect, the support and one of the privileged alibis. It has been one with the phallocentric tradition," says Cixous.[10] Our nostalgia for a "whole" self is less a nostalgia for origins than it is for the parts of our female memory that have been violently blanked out by patriarchy. I sometimes imagine "whole" as representing **w** (for women's difference, the unspoken) + **hole** (as our sex is frequently referred to by men). French-language women have been writing texts which seem to gush angrily forth out of these memory blanks. Québec writer France Théoret's *Bloody Mary* is a stunning instance of this. And Marguerite Duras says that while working, she often suddenly comes across a blank or gap in memory which she believes to be a vehement subconscious refusal of syntax, a sweeping away of syntax, the better to find something that lies behind.[11]

It seems impossible, then—if we are to find ways of speaking, seeing, better suited to our needs—to avoid the story's running over into poetry, derivative of journal, embracing theory. The latter is important, because then it's a feminist hand that guides us in the exploration of the shape of our desire. Our very knowledge that we as writers need this exploration springs from our experience of the feminist community. Again theory (root: the Greek word for look on, contemplate) is required for our work to move forward from the fragments and other forms of writing surfacing behind history's veil of silence. Because, to reflect our difference, these fragments have to be pierced by new conceptions (collectively worked out) of time, space and continuity.

Yet, still I'm saying "story." "Story," because while deconstructing the myths about us, the silence, in our writing, we're also involved in reconstructing the historically absent female subject. "Story," because in the telling, a line of narrative is woven intertextually, encompassing elements of a community, past and present (The story, they say, is 40,000 years old.) "Story," especially (for me) because the form implies a certain magic leading to any possibility. "Story": it doesn't matter if it's long or short.

"Story"—a woman's form.

Vancouver, 1983

NOTES

1 Claudine Herrmann, *Les Voleuses de langue* (Paris: Les Editions des Femmes, 1976), p. 9 (trans. Gail Scott).

2 Viviane Forrester, *La Violence du calme* (Paris: Les Editions du Seuil, 1980), p. 17.

3 Virginia Woolf, *A Room of One's Own* (1929; Harmondsworth: Penguin, 1945), pp. 77-78.

4 Julio Cortazar, interview, *Nuit Blanche,* No. 6 (Spring-Summer, 1982).

5 Marguerite Duras (and Xavière Gauthier), *Les Parleuses* (Paris: Les Editions de Minuit, 1974), p. 11 (trans. Gail Scott).

6 Claire Lejeune, "L'écriture et l'irréférence" (article, but place of publication unknown).

7 Hélène Cixous, "The Laugh of the Medusa," trans. Keith Cohen and Paula Cohen, *New French Feminisms,* ed. Elaine Marks and Isabelle de Courtivron (New York: Schocken, 1981), p. 245.

8 This figure is described in Luce Irigaray's writing, notably in *Ce Sexe qui n'en est pas un* (Paris: Les Editions de Minuit, 1977).

9 Duras, p. 49.

10 Cixous, p. 250.

11 Duras, p. 12.

PARAGRAPHS BLOWING
ON A LINE

The novel is the fiction form that most forces the writer to rub against the "real." By "real" I mean that "universal" represented by society's institutions: the practice of politics, of systems of law, education, etc. A woman, it seems to me, can write a short story, a poem, that might choose to remain in the margin of this apparent "universal"—the society of patriarchy's creation. Not unaffected by it, of course, but, on the immediate surface of the writing, unconcerned. Something in the novel, however, leads one to acknowledge this "universal," even if only to reject it. Perhaps it is the novel's length, a length which requires one to engage narrative, that is, to find some thread to which the reader might cling, or touch back on—no matter how experimental, no matter how it diverges in form along the way. And this thread has a historicity about it, even if it's broken or displaced or perverted, which implies reference to the "universal." A novel so experimental as to refuse this thread still finds itself acknowledging, in its very struggle against it, the pull towards this thread.

Yet, women deeply involved with new forms of women's writing still attempt the novel. Perhaps the reason is that we need that chance, occasionally, to check out where we are in terms of the "universal," to see if we are capable of creating another "universal," to see if we even want to pose the question that way. I doubt very much we do....

SITTING AT A CAFE table, in a park, on a bus, the notes I take that will later become prose, have ... the sound of poetry. So why must they become sentences become narrative? Why must I get involved with this forward movement of time the novel seems to require, when the voice of the notes, the woman's voice beckons me towards poetry?

This diary was written over the years I worked on my novel *Heroine*. A diary that has been condensed, entries altered, renumbered: a fake diary in a sense. Written often in a café with a blue floor, where, for awhile on the café wall, hung the perfect iconography for a woman struggling with the novel form: a poster of a sailor with a drawn knife standing under the tower of Pisa—which had become a *precariously leaning penis.*

ENTRY 1

The woman artist exists. I will make her exist within the city which I shall represent as a crazy stabbing sensibility (... the knife in the stomach . . . put your finger where it hurts . . . there's such a hole to fill).

But what's the story? And how shall I write it so the inner voice does not overwhelm the external interplay between her, the city, her, politics, her and her friends. And why do I see a dichotomy between the two (her excessive inner voice and the "real")?

ENTRY 2

When I think "novel" the images flood in on me from the exterior (the city); from memory, too. I can't believe their richness: the street images deeply musical. The heroine washed over by the poetry—and the voraciousness—of the city. The warm wind of an August night (smelling of dust and grease); the guy coming at her out of the darkened flower market. A background of clashes of cars. Hundreds of tires stacked against a wall. Rhythmic, discordant. I write, but I'm writing round in circles. Often uncut by periods (sentences). I love this poetic confrontation with language. But the novel requires some attempt at making sense. Some forward movement, presumably encapsuled in grammatical units of time represented by the sentence. Is not a novel above all a recording of moving (changing) time?

ENTRY 3

In the blue café. Outside the snow is falling. The rain is falling. *The tears are falling.* My voice confused with some country-and-western song line coming over the radio. My . . . melodrama threatening to take over the story line. Woman's "bathos" (*ludicrous descent from the elevated to the common in writing or speech*) versus the patriarchal "pathos" (*that quality in speech, writing, music, or artistic representation which excites a feeling of pity or sadness*)? But a feminist can't write melodrama—unless she finds some critical approach to the writing of it. And to acknowledge whatever melodrama means in our lives (I'm sick of denials, fed-up with the cardboard feminist, the utopian lesbian), requires fictional devices. A little perversion perhaps? In the opening scene she's in a bathtub remembering a devastating love affair with a trendy left leader. And she likes the embrace of cold enamel (then warm water) better than the lover's presence. Hopefully this twist (the inner voice that both wants and refuses love) will make her acceptable from a feminist point of view.

ENTRY 4

Still not the semblance of a narrative, only the craziest images. Like, the loved one sitting in the restaurant under a picture of a cross in a bleeding loaf of bread. And behind the window-pane, the mountain, that round breastlike hump, also with its cross. Images, which, in their contradictions, seem to point boisterously to movement towards some other meaning. Images which need, at the very least, to be transformed into an anecdote to string, among others, along a story line.

But all I see is my character: a woman in a bath. An empty bath, but she's oblivious, for she's masturbating under a jet of water. I have to find a narrative way to give her meaning. Some plot to tie together the memories floating past her in the steam, not only the lost love, but also the dissolution of certain political dreams in what she knows already will be the Yuppie decade (the 80s). And, to relate these somehow to the images from the "exterior," the street. Such as that domed-shaped café and women in cloche-shaped hats because there's an ambience of mid-30s Berlin in the air (this strange repetitive movement of time). Spoons playing against long-stemmed glasses and the high voice of the waitress. Fragments of her best friend, Marie, in her apartment, dropping pot on the floor and saying (because she is order where the main character is chaos): "je ferai le ménage demain." Her repugnance of disor-der coming from generations of Québécois women ordering the chaos of colonization.

A bell in my head says Produce, produce. But I can't just sit down and write a novel about X. It all happens in the process of writing. I agree with Barthes that writing has to do with the body's pursuing *its own ideas—for my body does not have the same ideas I do.*

ENTRY 5

In the blue café, the poster with the sailor under the leaning tower of penis is still on the wall. Below it sits a gay man with a sublimely "feminine" way of beaming out from under his curly eyelashes. So radically ambiguous, he could never be fitted into the good consciousness of a straight narrative. I mean, a narrative that puts one foot carefully down in front of the other, never slipping, never sliding, never challenging morality.

But what, exactly, is the problem with narrative time for my heroine? In the bath time flies (I think I'll leave her there for several hours)—yet, also seems not to move (as is often the case in severe situations of depression—for she's depressed). I have to find a form to reflect this double movement. It has something to do with trying to confront past and present at once. I don't only want her memories, i.e., how she got into the tub. But also for the text to have a running self-reflexive commentary about now. As in a kind of poetic essay about women today; or in the way poets insert the everyday in their texts.

Of course, both the self-reflexive and the "poetic voice" implied by the present tense appear to close some of the space between writer and text. Poets generally feel no need to hide behind fictional characters. With fiction, it's different. Even so, people will say "it's autobiography, like all first novels." Odd how many women keep writing "first novels" over and over again. In Québec, we've been saying that women, in writing their own gendered voices, are creating a "real" that has to date existed only as fiction created by males.

ENTRY 6

It's a bright crisp winter day. I keep writing, writing, but can't get past those first pages that came to me as a song in the blue café the other day. The music of the words balancing her guilt, her dilettantism. She's a "revolutionary" but also the petty bourgeois, the imperfect feminist and the badly-loved woman—although she doesn't see that at first. Still, she has her ideals, which I'll have to work on a little. Now, I find it impossible to recapture the way the sentences swing between past and present, between "inner" and "outer." The beauty of her nostalgia is transformed to a heavy sadness which doesn't satisfy me at all.

Ha, if I just gave into the pull of melodrama, *then* I'd have a story: The Three Stages of Love:

1. Before: Country girl comes to the city in search of freedom.

2. During: Of course there would be the twist that the love affair, whether failed or successful, is her fall—although in her eyes, and in the world's, the great moment also of validation and eroticism.

3. After: But then, here again, the problem with the narrative: she behaving "doubly" in a kind of attraction / repulsion towards the love object, ending up wallowing in a destructive inability to choose. *Une obsession est le point de bifurcation entre deux alternatifs,* a Québécois friend said once. The fork in her road possibly leading two different ways: the heterosexual, consumed by her love for the male; or the free woman, possibly lesbian? Is the work of the novel to choose? Or is it to follow the thread of obsession, wherever it goes? What if her inability to choose results in her becoming like the grey woman, a stunning "baglady" who gets more and more integrated into the tapestry of the city.

If this character ends up as part of a tapestry, in other words not unary, neatly resolved, she will fragment the novel form!

ENTRY 7

What dissatisfies me about her sadness is that she can't just be lying in the tub lamenting her problems (even love as she sees it is a "luxury" compared to what many third-world women are experiencing) while the rest of the world goes to hell. There would be no point in adopting the novel form if I were not aiming to reflect both her interior world and the "universal" questions of an epoch. For example, the issue of revolutionary social change—incarnated by the events in Poland (late 70s)—might show how slant the issue of revolutionary purity appeared to the women comrades of the left group she joined. For in Poland the Solidarity movement, which the male comrades hoped would lead to a new type of revolution within the socialist state, remained Catholic and patriarchal.

Again, the issue is form. The left has long held up Brecht as the solution. It's true, the Brechtian model was greatly ahead of the "direct representation" model of social realism in the way his characters become analogies of social problems, Mother Courage, for example. But the feminine 'I' still gets crushed. And it's already crushed a priori (in my imagining of my heroine) by politics, by her left lover, as well as by patriarchy. The first pages, that came to me so magically here in the blue café, work inasmuch as I write to my most inner voice, yet the "outside" things are present. It seems to depend on the way sentences, paragraphs, slip from one to the other.

And what do do with this very unfeminist idea my heroine seems to have that the past always seems best? The histrionics sometimes read rather well in the notes: *His infidelity finally made me break down and cry. At last I was distraught enough to express my hysterics (it was a little forced, grant it. I shut myself in the bathroom and painted my naked body with lipstick. Then I went out and told him I was now ready to seduce our friend, K.). But I could not put out my arms to be comforted by his emotional incompetence. Life was a long lesson of repression in that sense. Men were always taking me away from a certain kind of self-expression—at the same time their presence solicited it from me.*

ENTRY 8

On the wall of the blue café, a huge poster advertising the Chantal Akerman film *Toute Une Nuit*. A woman in a midnight-blue dress, 40s style, high heels. Walking the streets of a Belgian city with other women, and their men, almost wordlessly (the film has very little script). Women in couples, walking in their high heels, out for a gala evening which, to the viewer, becomes more and more exhausting. The film becoming both a social commentary on middle-class sex roles, as well as leaving the spaces (due to the silences?) for the viewer to feel, imagine, the inner thoughts of these women. So that the viewer participates in closing the gap between woman's inner and outer experience.

If only I could find a way to do this in words, to make possible a reading other than the one necessarily arising from the author's being stuck—as I am—in the writer / narrator / novel subject relationship. But if I distanced from her in the more conventional way, where the author floats overhead, looking down at her, how would I get back into her? It's her voice I want to explore; rather than being out there in culture looking down on her.

Meanwhile, I'm failing to relate to my poor secondary characters. Oddly, uninvited, almost mythical characters have stepped in, and are taking up more space than the minor secondary characters (the comrades, etc.). One is a Black man looking through a telescope on the mountain. I have no idea who he is or what he is doing there. And the grey woman, who has come over from an older unpublished manuscript. Then there is this person my heroine addresses in moments of great excitement, called Sepia. Who or what is Sepia? Memory perhaps, but coloured like an old photo, the sepia tint taking away the sharp contrast between black and white. There is something dreamlike about this Sepia. She seems to represent an ideal of perfection. Like the moment of "love" in a Northern European town, that my heroine remembers through a photo taken of her and her ex-lover. The photo lays now on a stool by her tub.

ENTRY 9

No one would dare call *The Sorrows of Young Werther* melodrama. Yet, imagine a woman trying to write a story of such ...
hysterical obsession with the love object. A love so unbear-
able, young Werther had to kill himself.

It's a fact that there's something a little off about her relationship to this ... melodrama. What if she is only participating
in it as a way to cope? We all have memories of participating in
various not-quite-appropriate narratives, the better to live up
to an image projected on us from outside. Maybe melodrama
is another form of fake narrative to carry one through
difficulty. For a period in my life I got hooked on the soaps,
precisely when I was trying to play a female role in which I no
longer believed. So there was a kind of distance from my own
gestures. My life organized into tableaux, representing not an
inner "real" but only what appeared to be happening on the
surface.

Like in the soaps, my heroine's story might involve an
almost theatrical repetition of emotions. Maybe using a repetitive image, like Proust's bell ringing when Swann enters the
garden gate, to give a critical distance to the "story."

The whole novel could proceed as a series of her bird's-eye
views from the bathtub. This would be a way of integrating
different times, levels of consciousness: her nostalgia and a
commentary produced by the narrator's feminist consciousness. Except I want this to be exploration, not prescriptive
writing. All language has to be seen as material to work on. In
Finnegan's Wake too there is the "tale of the tub" (tubloid?),
linked both *to the cabbalistic signification of letters and the
psychological imperative of literature.* These words excite me
so much for writing. That a tale quits a "normal" narrative line
to examine the cabbalistic signification of letters, and how that
fits into a process that resembles (but is not) psychoanalysis.
That letters might have cabbalistic signification. Wow.

ENTRY 10

Outside the blue café, a woman passes with bright orange earrings, beautifully-cut aubergine hair, a short skirt over tights with foot-straps and pointy shoes. Very French. And I'm thinking another problem with my heroine is that she doesn't "possess" Montréal. She's on the outside edge, with snow, romantic, overdetermined, falling like syrup. Yes, a cliché—because she's English—albeit cut up, troubled by rock, country, etc. The move to transgress her English-Canadian parents' goal for her (to marry a nice boy and settle down somewhere in Ontario) is to enter *la cité*. French is *la cité* is also transgression. Which makes coming down to Montréal a very different thing than going to Toronto. Exacerbates her (poetic) voice, separates her too from the weight of the narrative (tradition) of her own culture. Partly because poetry has been *revendicative* in Québec; partly because feminists here transformed the conjuncture between *la modernité* and feminism into a prose form called *le récit,* located somewhere between the novel and *l'écriture* (the text).

But to acknowledge this is to open even wider the space between her and the "real." *Et comment constituer un sujet du roman qui tente de parler de deux pôles opposés simultanément?* The cultural polarities only adding to the other oppositions, so there seems little possibility of comforting the fear and tentativeness in her voice. The "soap-flakes" conversations between him & her, the interior monologue which is really a dialogue among the different parts of herself (and her best friend, Marie, who may turn out to represent the feminist discourse), her fear of becoming like the older homeless women, all exclude a straightforward resolution of the story. Yet, paradoxically, to move on, I have to stop being afraid of the novel. Of her / my profound sense of failure in relationships.

Sitting in HJ's living room I feel I talk too much. Make too many self-conscious little comments. The continuing sense of relationship failure resembling my incapacity to finish a novel. I have a recurring dream of living in my parent's house, getting older and older yet unable to move. With a sense of unbelievable depression, I paint my childhood room one more time.

ENTRY 11

She sees the present as a great tear, a great rip in the surface of things: the gap of which is at first impossible for her to move across (... *does not thinking seek forever to clamp a dressing over the gaping and violent wound of the impossibility of thought ...?*).[1] It is awareness of this that makes linear narrative impossible. A virtually *tragic* awareness, for the writing "I," which the modernists began to "deconstruct" as they recognized that gap (accepted to give up power) has, in her case, been "deconstructed" a priori by social conditions. She is not only split between the self and the "real," but also within the self: between wife, lover, at worst, baglady, at best, free woman ... as she was before the affair and ... as she may be after. The overdetermined illusiveness of her-self reminds me of those magazines where they do her over into the after woman, the after woman being the hardest of the two to achieve and especially to maintain.

So the question becomes how to write across the almost ... hysterical . . . overdetermination of her gaps. A feminist film critic suggests women's new narrative should move "beyond deconstruction to reconstruction," to learn how to "manipulate the recognized dominating discourses so as to begin to free ourselves *through* rather than beyond them." As an example, she recommends a return to melodrama, which she calls narrative at its most hysterical. And Luce Irigaray says that in the potential lurking behind the hysterical mask lies the woman's great reserve for revolt. The mask also protects her inner self from patriarchy. Obviously, feminism, in its sense of creating conditions in which she may be *herself-defined,* offers another pole of attraction for the psyche of a woman obsessed.

Thanks to those first pages written in the blue café (written, uncomfortably performance-like, under the stare of a shy blond man at another table), I am beginning to see what her internal grammar does to the sentence, the paragraph, how the paragraphs "slip," and the sentences, to reflect this turbulent inner resonance.

The "shy" blond man got up and asked me if I was a translator.

ENTRY 12

People are lined up for the cinema at the back of the blue café to see Werner Schroeter's *Répétition Générale*. It's a film about an alternative theatre festival at Nancy, brilliantly and subversively combining various genres. Example, using "documentary" images from the carnival of plays as a commentary on our times, as well as interjecting a bit of the director's autobiographical commentary, a bit of a love story that might be his personal fiction, and even Prometheus on a roof providing a deconstructed mythological angle on the whole thing. I envy people who work with visual images (performance artists, film-makers, installation artists). The audience seems to accept that visual images can "slip," may have multiple meaning, whereas writers, expecially those working in prose, can easily be trapped in the preconceived notions ascribed to words by ideology.

ENTRY 13

Were I to have accepted ages ago to write this in fragments, it would be finished by now. But I persist in feeling strongly it should be a "novel" or at least have the appearance thereof. To reach for that plot that will in some way gather all the threads together, work out her contradictions, all in the context of dealing with several of the key issues of our time. In short, I dream of finding the form for a character who is *typical of her generation*—as a male artist advised me once.

Can a woman be *typical* of her generation?

Also, it's as old as human memory, the desire for story which is after all an attempt to put order in our lives, to understand—a need women certainly feel today. Maybe my resistance to the narrative conventions of the novel have to do with what I think of as its Protestant qualities: its earnest representation of the "real," its greed for action, its preference for the concrete over the philosophical.

A compromise might be possible: structuring the story by means of the fluctuations in her ... (dare I?) hysterical voice. The use of the voice invoking a poetic meaning in excess of the sentence. But the forward movement of the healing process, i.e., her coming-to-awareness of what needs to be changed, displaced in her context in order to come through the labyrinth, invoking the novel. The opening scenes of her in the bath are very mad, for she's remembering it all at once. Then relative calm: her (bath) mood altered by remembering moments of euphoria. This plot, the plot of her obsession, dealt with *blow by blow*. But it's clearly only a thread of the whole novel: the memory of each meeting is framed by her attempts in the tub to create a "present." Juxtaposing the woman from the past (memories, perhaps recorded in a diary) in relation to the "now" woman, she who is commenting on the situation of disintegrating advanced capitalism which keeps reviving like a spent prick, featuring as its great achievement in personal relations: the royal couple and its apex of creation: the nuclear family.

And I just wrote the relationship can be dealt with *blow by blow*. Blows: violent and unusual interruptions in her narrative texture—which texture the writing is hopefully starting to discover. More and more I intuit that it has to do with starting from a negative point: a crushed ego that doesn't see its boundaries. Except who ever heard of a novel hero / ine with a crushed ego? You might say Proust's or Kafka's heros—yet little Marcel, at least, despite his insecurities, has a giant ego. Another problem: *écrire un roman, c'est se constituer comme sujet....* (Québécois writer Lise Gauvin).

ENTRY 14

Milan Kundera: *the novel is an interrogative meditation of experience.* Whose experience? But I am not proposing the opposite of that cool meditation either—even if my promiscuous relationship with my narrator still risks being too sticky. Example, I am currently suffering from a sinus problem and immediately, I want to add this to the litany of problems suffered by the woman in the bath. She can't smell, so she's afraid to go near anyone. Because she might smell; or they might. Then things get worse. Her nose runs constantly. She's allergic to everything, including herself. *She feels like the hooker she saw going by Dapper Dan's along Ste. Catherine in the slush. She had red spots on her face. Her blonde hair, pulled back tight in a pony tail, was greasy, her clothes mussed. As if she had been held prisoner in a downtown hotel for too long. She walked through the slush, through the traffic, heading east as if nothing could stop her. Heading towards a fixed point, her delicate pointed hooker boots ruined by the damp snow. Maybe overdue for a shot of something to help her forget everything that happened to her.*

If I were a painter I could get the charge of subjectivity right, painting over it until it became "art" at the same time as I caressed it (her). As in the succinctly brushed watercolours of Virginia Woolf; or Jane Bowles' bright bits of colour floating chaotically in the clear air; or Djuna Barnes' black with the odd bits of circus red; or the shadowlessness of Nicole Brossard's writing (is it the absence of the past for her that makes her writing *sans ombres* as F.T. says?) In fact, I imagine this novel as having the sepia tint of a photograph with occasional touches of colour—like when you paint on a black-and-white photo. The colour being the immediacy of her commentary, of what she wilfully adds to the image to make it *hers*, to make it radically different from *his* image. That shot of them leaning together in the Northern European courtyard, for example. The trick being to find the potentially moving point (Barthes' punctum) in the "still lifes" taken by him that are on the stool by her tub. The point that draws her perception beyond his framing of the image into a new story. She's working from a negative (reading) of these images blowing on his (story) line, images she will take off and arrange her own way. At first his black-and-white images are what she wanted to climb into. Where she fled obsessively—for comfort. I need to extract the hope (which she at first believes is represented by him) from the obsession.

The triumph in the novel is only that the obsession grows smaller. The melodrama gets reduced. A minor triumph. She will just integrate it in all its beauty and its pain, like an oyster integrates a pearl.

ENTRY 15

If I were to hang my "negatives" on the line in a new chapter order, it would be:

1. Sepia (the café on The Main with him sitting under a bleeding loaf of bread).

2. The Dream Layer (*l'étreinte* in the Northern European courtyard).

3. Euphoria and the New Order of the Revolutionary Couple (a scene from their apartment).

4. The Resentment (she tries to escape into art).

5. Feminism (she leaves the revolutionary organization in a long skirt).

6. The Rupture (the last wait on the balcony).

7. Under the Line of Pain.

But it's odd how one can't will order even by writing it down. For Under the Line of Pain is *not* chapter 7. It's there all the time, through her whole night of remembering "what happened." A thick black line she drew in her diary the day she decided to reconcile with him. But where does it start? Not necessarily with the line of melodrama, for the pain was in her before the love story ever started. And the author herself gets caught up in the story, is wounded by it—and also transformed. To help me keep it framed with some kind of analysis, my notes should include a few comments every week about now, this space and time, my grasping of it. It makes me so angry certain feminists prefer to deny the pain, glossing over it. Have they forgotten Barnes' terror of abandonment? Woolf's terror of schizophrenia? Jane Bowles ordering whiskey after whiskey until she collapses in Montréal Central Station....

The comrades referred (reductively) to the terror as *la misère sexuelle*. This lack of love walking on The Main thinking: I can't write another word untouched. Feeling guilty about my existence. Does someone as little productive as me even deserve to eat?

Then I sit in the blue café and for the wrong reasons feel better. Because, I feel superior to the elderly artsy couple at the next table.... Her: "What do you want to eat dear?" Him: "Let me tell you about the (university) art department. It's the best year and they would like to cut the budget." Is that all there is? Do we all end up reducing our ideals so? Politics as an obsession of our generation—now overlaid with the "fight" for survival-with-a-decent-lifestyle.

ENTRY 16

Outside the window of the blue café, it is snowing, always snowing. In the dim grey light across the street a man (with the beginning of multiple sclerosis?) takes small, obviously painful steps. At the next table someone is telling a story about a woman lawyer, a brilliant criminal lawyer who fell in love with one of her clients and ended up following him to a foreign country. There he treated her . . . criminally. Finally she came back, her professional credibility destroyed. Then her mother, whom she dearly loved, died. She spent months wrapped in her mother's things, rocking in her mother's chair.

I can't resist the texture offered by a voice like hers. I imagine it swinging from a poetic excess of words, context, to a feigned control (deferring to some sort of borrowed narrative). The latter with an apparently smooth surface, but with such spaces between the words as to imply another meaning. This is the real meaning of *writing over the top:* The text, the writing becomes a kind of third voice, not the author or the narrator, but the voice of the author/narrator subsumed (as opposed to commenting from a distance as in a more traditional narrative) into the object of the narration. Jane Bowles writes better in this third voice than anyone else. She's found a way to leave behind the univocal author, so that the writing subject exists at the point where the inner and outer voices meet. Instead of a cold distant reading, you get a maddening buzzing effect.

But, again I've conjured up a vision of hysteria, reviving in me the fear that if I fiddle with it too closely, I will end up with writing that is neither "art" nor "feminist." *L'hystérie, c'est l'oeuvre d'art manqué,* Philippe Sollers said somewhere. Perhaps referring to the difficulty of synthesis psychology books claim characterizes hysterical mental processes. The surrealists, contrary to Sollers, thought the hysterical hallucination was the seminal vision for an artist. Of course, the symptoms were generally displayed by the muse and synthesized by the male artist. Breton's Nadja being a prime example of this.

ENTRY 17

The world races towards destruction. If one were to keep a daily record of potential environmental / war disasters coming over the radio in the blue café, every other gesture would seem futile. Nuclear waste problems, the greenhouse factor, famine.

And in the midst of it all, I'm trying to create a *subject* with a bathtub for a setting. A tissue of the author, the woman's body and the would-be writer (whom the narrator is creating), working their way out of the tub. Starting with the long come. Can anything be more "present" than the spasm of orgasm? True, the small flutters are also absence, absence that heightens clarity of vision the minute after. Bit by bit the bathroom is revealed. It contains *le trame* of her current life. The place where the struggle goes on between repression and the search for integrity (I almost said, between *representation* and the search for integrity), between hysteria and . . . whatever lies at the other side of that labyrinth.

What is the present, anyway, but a defence against memory? At least, a defence against the nostalgic effects of memory: the narrator has to defend herself against the character she has created for whom "the past always seems best." It is ironic that despite the fuzzing of her boundaries with the author, in terms of what she thinks, I shall clearly, wilfully, have to invent this narrator as I go along. The invention must be the result of her movement through language though, and not the inverse. *To do this is to assume that what she thinks is important. And this assumption and this invention are my real concessions to the novel form.*

I still see the secondary characters in crazy, exuberant images. The male lover is walking down a country road. The fields are dark green and the sky ink blue. A field of excited Holsteins gather round, moving after him.

Her relationship to the female characters is more symbiotic. Like waking up in the sun, feeling the skin of his arm, then knowing it's the other, the rival, and not she, the heroine, who feels it now. So she projects her own soap opera onto the rival (but the rival has been complicit)—the boundaries between the two of them breaking down. My heroine is not only a woman of many self-images, but is also part of the other women she is close to. The women she loves and hates.

ENTRY 18

In the blue café. Bessie Smith is singing *nobody cares for me.* Reminding me that the song form seems closest to the voice / body proximity I want to evoke in my writing. The novel a jazz counterpoint with all those notes floating around in the air and every so often you pick out a melody to help it "move forward" a little. Catching what you catch. Of the life in restaurants that have *"mets canadiens"* written over the door. Of the thin layer of civilization we, who are still a fairly provincial people, have donned. The working class in the city with its country-and-western undertones

In fact, the heroine has a present / absent bodily relationship to this context. The streets are a spectacle which her body takes in. The female body, fragmented, in pain, its cells reaching out to all the other fragmented, pained bodies, the women, the poor, the effects of *les restes de colonization,* is sometimes literally splayed over the city. Bodies talking. Taking refuge in the warmth and safety of cafés. The little indulgences (too much coffee) against this pain, that are killing her.

She also, somewhat perversely, perceives her body as absence inasmuch as it speaks a minority language in the Québec context (albeit the traditional language of the bosses).

It is limited, outside of where things are really at. Everything happens in French. And my narrator prefers that the meaning be in another language. For she has consciously chosen her minority situation—which is very different than being colonized, when meaning happens in the other language and it's out of your power to do anything about it. Her political consciousness doesn't prevent her from being jealous of Maurice, the court clerk, whose mother stabbed him in Abitibi, the "natural" poet for whom the pain was so great (and the confidence so little) he became middle class. To "join" *la cité* she has to join the revolution or not exist. The "present" can only be represented by some sort of social insertion, or a lucid refusal of it, which is the same thing. Her tremendous nostalgia for the lost love affair in that sense is significant, because it was the only previous incident where her inner self with all its lust for culture, freedom, sexual satisfaction and revolt came (momentarily, in the first throes of that love) together with her outer self. Her desire to repeat that past moment in time *as if nothing had changed* is what gets her stuck. What she is inventing is a new lucidity regarding everyday life, "now," as a woman on her own terms. And it can only be invented as she speaks (writes) it.

Otherwise, she's just a female figure out there dressed up and walking. Attracted like a magnet towards the tragic of the street: the junkie family; the blond musician in love with his sister. His hair is turning white from too much coke.

ENTRY 20

I met a woman like my heroine at an extremely violent pornography film put on by an anti-porn feminist group. I had stepped out for a cigarette; she, because she couldn't take it. At first she, a beautiful redhead from Newfoundland, mocked the male lust for the chained woman in the film. But suddenly the mask slipped, and she said, kind of offhand, that she was a rape victim. Said she was going to have to move from her rooming house because the landlord was after her. She's put a chain on her door. Walking down the street on the way here, two guys drove up on the sidewalk trying "to get her." They even backed up.

My heroine, too, comes to this city to put on a mask of greater sophistication (replacing the nice-girl mask one has to wear in a small town, except in the small town she kept slipping, being a kind of whore or perceiving herself as such. Unable to handle the overwhelming sexual demand). Anyway, now I see the possibility of a more suitable order to the text, fluctuating between her excesses, covered at first by her attempts at borrowed narrative, but becoming more "centred" with the intervention of the feminist voice (her own and others). So,

—coming to the city: a place to have fun. The seduction. The fear / excitement of whatever comes after lighting up the first cigarette of the morning. The delicious, almost self-destructive desire to be constantly living "on the edge." Partly kept afloat by her illusion of being in a perfect couple.

—the crescendo of breaking out of the couple, which is breaking out of another mask she has adopted. Leading up to his "paying her back" for her infidelities, while she slowly sinks below the line of pain. Lucidly, for the writing in her diary is a record she will finally reorganize, refrain, to distance herself from this distress. Her attempt to write across the gap to the world outside and its effects on her. Among others, to catch exactly the moment when things change. When people go from the sandals of the 60s to the high heels of the later 70s, the coming of Yuppiedom. And what happens in the mind. How people give in to greed and power. Even the "revs." The relative inconsequence of her "suffering" in the context of the third world, which is present on her TV.

—the feminist "mask," and in it she begins to believe that only with women can she watch/participate in this spectacle without total disintegration.

ENTRY 21

I think I'm finding a form to permit me to write what Carla Harryman calls the middle ground . . . *where what's enlarged (subjective) and what's reduced (external) by speaking gather.*[2] At least inasmuch as I manage to protect the voice of the text from bending to a traditional narrative line. Indeed, the moment she can't forget is the moment she tried to get into the narrative. Signaled in her diary by that thick black line of pain, drawn when she decided to force herself back into a relationship about which (deep down) she had serious reservations. Because it represented, somehow, survival. Between him and the baglady, given the depth of her despondency, she could see nothing but an abyss. But as she knew from the start it wouldn't work, and consequently did everything for it not to work: it was a false line.

On the other hand, I can't keep myself from imagining a character in which the excesses of pain and ecstasy, as well as her "theoretical" rumination on a "solution" are … credible. Another concession to the novel. Credible aesthetically rather than politically, however. Like Nietzsche's Apollonian artist trying to deliver the spectator (herself) from her own Dionysian extravagance through the process of creation. But her resultant "collage" still harkens greatly to the unconscious, to song in the Dionysian sense, to the mother perhaps. The Nietzschean analogy in this sense is not perfect.

Could this character, so birdlike, infinitely poetic, beautiful, chaotic . . . and, ultimately, wise . . . emerge as anything but an artist? Her voice pitched in a tone of *Je ne regrette rien*. In constant movement from one café to another, from place to place. Between the "phallic battering" of a society stacked against women, and her labyrinthine voyage through memory and the present. *More easily rendered in a sonata than in a novel,* to quote the tub-woman.

ENTRY 22

Virginia Woolf complained that English novelists frequently spell out that *one way is right and the other way is wrong.* Protestant guilt to maintain genre. But how does guilt function precisely in writing this novel? The guilt which has always been a tangible component of my awareness. Losing my bracelet and wondering what I've been punished for. Too guilty to ever enjoy "now." Always waiting for the cycle to peak, for things to take a turn for the worse. And the biggest guilt of all: the one which says I'll be punished for pleasure in love. In the novel, the man is Beau. Tenderly progressive. And she? In the shadow of the hooker. Who's everywhere.

> *dada dadadada*
> *dada dadadada*
> *we're all guilty*
> *we're all guilty*
> *we're all guilty of love*

Even feminism can become a factor of guilt. This is complicated because the synthesis is in some sense made possible by feminist discourse. But feminism tends to want to deny madness, tending always towards a new feminist norm. It wants her to get rid of her pessimism, her melancholy.

ENTRY 23

I'm getting a clearer picture of her, she's becoming, a fictional character who belongs to the streets of the city. I'm the voyeur, who, drawing a curtain, reaches out to look at life in the park. The paradox is feeling that in creating her I'm winning the uphill struggle against my own wimpy ego. That I'm hearing my own voice more and more as I write her. And that she in turn is also a voice altered, strengthened by the other women in her milieu.

ENTRY 24

In the blue café, really called Café Méliès, after the founder of the French cinema, a lover of the fantastical.... Trying to write quite a long passage now on the warmest period, the period of great complicity among women. That high watermark of feminism (late 70s) when the restaurants for the first time were full of women in pairs, in groups. (One wonders what the men did during that period.) When one was experimenting, at last, with trusting women first. And the ambiguous sexuality in the air, the fading of the line between lesbian and straight. This is the period in the novel, in her remembering, where she "writes over the top" quite easily, as if from a new ethic. It starts with her taking an easy stroll through the city, walking well back on her heels, knees slightly bent, pelvis forward. Yet all the time she feels a little like a poseur in her heady new self-assured garb, as if this isn't quite it either. For she will, she must face her own particular madness, her own particular pain. To pass through it *in words*. To "accept" her hysteria as not only negative; as an adventure. And pass through it.

In the projection room at the back of the café, they are showing Cocteau's *Orpheus*. The woman in it reminds her of her best friend Marie, with her 40s-style nipped-in waist and black gloves. Marie is the best kind of feminist, committed, yet capable of facing the *inevitable*.

ENTRY 25

During this whole process I have been caught between the need to accomplish this thing, which is both to posit some new kind of subject and to have the sense of being a subject myself; and yet to resist repeating, by creating a "feminist narrative," what Barthes calls ... the staging of a new "father," a new hierarchy of acceptable concepts. (*Every narrative (every unveiling of the truth) is a staging of the ... father.*) Maybe what my heroine discovers in trying to write her novel is only that the novel doesn't suit the (diffuse?) women's way of seeing things. Where there is closure (firm conclusions) in "straight writing" there are spaces, questions in hers. Even her anecdotes point to other possible representations, leave themselves open for reader intervention.

Still, given that my firm and conscious intention has been to counter (patriarchal) ideology in this process, the poststructuralist recipe for taking apart everything from the sentence to the author won't entirely do. Presumably I have to at least propose some other direction: language slips all around us. One's response to that is a question of the relationship between writing (what it comprises of consciousness) and body. Again to quote Barthes: *The text needs its shadow. This shadow is a bit of ideology, a bit of representation, a bit of subject: ghosts, pockets, traces, necessary clouds. Subversion must produce its own chiaroscuro.*

ENTRY 26

The Black tourist also walks through the city with a broader view of seasons, life, etc. The tub-talk, which frames the nostalgia, operates then within the larger frame of the Black man's telescope. Or, alternately, within the larger frame of the city, with the grey woman going through it. This double framing means that the scenes are separated by spaces, quite big ones, as if spit forth from a snowstorm. Spaces where, hopefully, interesting things might happen in the reader's mind. Spaces also offering an almost overdetermined means of separating me the author from the narrator Gail. At great distance is the

Black man on the mountain, who, looking through the telescope is creating his own order. She can't hear his thoughts. Nor those of the grey woman, who hardly speaks, except in nonsensical rhymes. But the grey woman calls up in her the desire to get out of it all, regardless of where that desire will take her. This temptation of utter solitude is reinforced by the heroine's feeling she's safe with nobody. And you can't survive in this society with nobody. *Jeanne Gilmore, a 33-year-old homeless woman, was found dead outside a hot air vent this morning. The temperature had dipped to 30 below overnight.*

In a funny kind of way, each section is both cinematic and photographic. The cinema, like her illusory narrative line, gives the illusion of time passing as in reality, of hence being in control, even when it hurts. The photo, on the other hand is so beautiful, so unreal. Like death.

ENTRY 27

And now I have to end this somewhere. Sitting in the blue café the other day, with a toothless, hungry woman outside the window, I had this idea (quickly discarded) that the story would end with my heroine sitting between two bagladies on The Main. A passerby would say to one of them: "your cunt smells." And the baglady (an ex-hippie) would reply, laughing toothlessly: "I can't wash it, I've got a molotov cocktail between my legs."

ENTRY 28

Some novelists claim their characters "come to them" like other voices. I'd have to say that about the structure, which always offers itself as a great revelation as a work is finishing. Of course, it doesn't "come to me" but is the fruit of my own hard thinking, and a considerable process of intertextuality, especially with other women's work. In fact, I am learning to trust "my feminist consciousness" enough to forget it when I write. It is something that is there partly as ballast, but ballast which by moments must be dangerously left behind, risked, in order to explore new depths. For my heroine has to finally face her pain, uncensored by her feminist consciousness. To really read her diary about those years where she felt dominated by feelings of victimization, anxiety. To stop repressing the writing, which is the only possibility of leaving a trace (a fleeting "presence" is better than none).

Yes, she will read her diary, deciding to use the writing in it as material, cut up, collage style, for the novel. She will get out of the tub and enter the city, thinking about these things. Walking through an early winter street, she will think of these things and of the women she may see, meet. And she will think of who / where she will be next. There will be no revelation, no blinding light on the road to Damascus. Just her walking through the snow. The novel will end with

She—

Montréal, 1982-86
Revised, 1988

NOTES

1 Gayatri Chakravorty Spivak, Translator's Preface to Jacques Derrida, *On Grammatology* (Baltimore: Johns Hopkins University Press, 1976).

2 Carla Harryman, *The Middle* (San Francisco: Gaz, 1983).

SPACES   LIKE   STAIRS

The end of genre, say the postmoderns. Yet we keep writing the (poetic) story, the (poetic) novel—further imbued with a little theory: i.e., commentary signifying that place where our writing processes consciously meet the politics of the women's community (as well as contemporary strategies for writing). This is the point in fiction where the rupture from our socialization in patriarchal society is marked most rationally. However, the novel, as a crossroads between two discourses (monologic and dialogic), remains ambivalent, theoretically. Hence, to mark the progress of each generation, the essay form is far from dead. Two challengers of genre earlier in the century produced Stein's How to Write, Woolf's Three Guineas. I also love the essays of Benjamin and Montaigne for their highly personal side. The two women authors "theorize" in a highly subjective manner on their own experience of writing while being clearly abreast of the progressive ideas of their times. The absence in their work of that deference to authority which obsesses authors of academic essays appeals to me. And the openness regarding form which that absence of deference permits.

A Québécois writer friend once said to me: One shouldn't have to change one's way of writing, no matter what one's writing. She meant criticism, journalism, fiction.... At the time, trained to be un écrivain de service (a journalist), I didn't totally understand. Now, I think, for me at any rate, it's precisely where the poetic and the personal enter the essay form that thought steps over its former boundaries.

what's   real?
the problem is   in the space
example rape is   a black card deck   chance   bad luck
as   normal product of patriarchal logic
what's   real
when the jolly female child is here   and the syntax (bound
pornographic image)   over there?
the problem is   in the space
after ten years of textual trying are we ready to say how to say
what   (our) real is?

she's repeating herself, the first time

   the problem is in the space   presently the problem is:
from what space can we best define our new culture   is
it in the space beyond the text   Nicole's utopia   or
in order to be "clear"   must we step back to older forms?
   the problem is in the space   the problem is in the
space between ideology and consciousness (old systems new
awareness   in this space was born the sentence)   the
problem is in the space between the conscious and the unconscious (once thought poetry's pure source)   out of
these two spaces in fusion has come the text   but what in
rising above the others has the text left?   has the text
left behind sense?   has the text left behind innocence
(words unbridled by self-censorship   what ideas are "in"
now asks the text?)   no, halt this way of thinking   what
ideas can be more relevant for me than those created as a
result of words circulating among (mostly) women?   can
one censor what makes one live?   yet   yet

perhaps the question is   how to keep the new space
open where women's culture rests   (that thin layer)   by
what forms might we make it resistant to the 80s avalanche of
co-option   yes how to state the facts when we are fiction
to be imaginative when our fiction is biography   when in
order not to sink in sadness our fiction must be theory
    you're repeating yourself, says a voice   just as
we're about to ask what space might our discursive writing
occupy, a voice says   you're repeating yourselves   but
but   can standards for a new culture be created if we say
things only once   what is beauty for us   excellence
may we mention only once (in the shadow of the phallus)
how the sustained pleasure of two lips leads to other than
dramatic climax   you're repeating yourselves, says the
voice   your illusions are dépassé   it's the 80s
    maybe the problem is in the space between male and fe-
male reading   we hear the masculine other with anxious ears
what's dangerous is he doesn't hear us   la femme tend
toujours *vers* dit Irigaray   sans retour à elle comme lieu
d'élaboration positive[1*]

prologue (working material)

IT happened one night. what happened? more important
how to write it? the movie starred Claudette Colbert and
Rock Hudson. in the black arch of starry sky the moon
shone. or, in the morning mist two lovers kissed and, and ...
IT transpired. but what was IT? naturally she the audience
saw IT other than he the audience did. he's one, on the inside looking in. she's herself and Claudette at the same time.

---

* Woman always tends towards the other, without returning to herself as a
place of positive elaboration (trans. G.S.).

as Rock takes her in his arms the freckled hands of several
men float by. Daddy's too. shhh. that was nothing. what were
we doing? I don't know Mommy because I don't know
what you call it. fun in the tub? seeing stars in the back yard?
I wanted Mommy to change my bed but he came. Daddy daddy cries the little girl in the new coat jumping up and down
beside the the smiling man while a camera draws the
line between acceptable (what you see) and unacceptable
seduction.

   (the young Freud said: incest creates hysteria in women.
but he had so many patients with that ailment he got em-
barrassed and had to change his theory. still, the question
rests: for the little girl as for every woman where's the
language line to separate real caring from exploitative
seduction?)

she's repeating herself, the second time

the problem is in the space   women sitting at a table
drinking wine from bottles with painted flowers on them
saying we must examine the theoretical gains of the
decade   we must write about our thin layer of culture in
order to move it forward   the essay is the form   the essay is
the way to write our new awareness into transformed
ideology laying out the argument from start to finish   but
one says: I can't think in a straight line   another: in fiction
my imagination lacks; in theory my autobiographical notes
destroy the facts
   the problem is in the space   if the mind works best
without those distinctions between reality / theory / fiction,
then the space has slipped from which the essay can spring
you're repeating yourself says the voice   the essay needs

logic to be clear   to avoid barbarism certain forms must be
borrowed from the dominating culture   at any rate there's
no danger of self-betrayal for you women are excellent at
translation   women are skilled at stepping into spaces
(forms) created by the patriarchal superego and cleverly subverting them
    true but above the reality line (as men define it) the
female body is left behind   two men meet in a university
department   they shake hands   the shoulders swagger
mr. s. I presume?   how goes the thesis?   the other plants
his feet more firmly on the ground   the beard waggles   it's
a phenomenal labour   but you know I already have a
publisher   next year I'm getting tenure
    the problem is in the space between our being   and their
saying   "la source du tragique consiste non dans
l'acte, mais dans la rencontre   (d'abord manquée, puis
graduellement réalisée) entre l'acte et le langage"* by
his own words Oedipus condemned himself   and went
down in history for soaring tragedy confirms existence   but
what if the body (act) is condemned by the language of the
other   (example bleeding on a white dress is disgustingly
inappropriate)   for as women the space between the act
and the other's language has been so great we never seemed
to close it   daddy saying do as I say not as I do   when
mother wanted neither of the two

epilogue (reworked material)

    the problem is in the space she's repeating herself again
the problem is in the space between herself and image she

---

*The source of the tragic is not in the act but in the meeting (at first failed
then gradually accomplished) between the act and language (trans. G.S.).

used to watch herself in the surrounding world of mirrors
which one was she hamlet had his words but ophelia slipped
silent down the river watching the mirrors she wondered
which one named her new woman amazon abandoned lover
mother daddy's girl french english every image had a
different way of talking every image had a different way of
walking she got so dizzy she had to stop looking
    yes that's the answer stop looking out at them the space
beyond the text is the new place one learns best the lessons
of the other culture when not bedazzled by the phallic
symbol as in djuna nicole gertrude maybe lesbian is easier
yes the old forms essay novel have moved forward maybe
two postmoderns one for women one for men ours circular
she's repeating herself again the problem is in the space
she's glad

Montréal, 1985

NOTES

1 Luce Irigaray, *Ethique de la différence sexuelle* (Paris: Editions
  de Minuit, 1984), p. 16.

2 Shoshana Felman, *Le Scandale du corps parlant* (Paris: Editions
  du Seuil, 1980), p. 130.

3

THE FEMINIST IN
THE WRITING

A FEMINIST AT
THE CARNIVAL

The debate about the relationship between art and politics spans generations and progressive movements without ever coming to a satisfactory "conclusion." Perhaps that's an indication of its health. How this relationship is named, defined, by different groups in different periods is, however, highly significant. In Québec, *for example,* l'écriture féministe *(feminist writing) has generally been rejected in favour of* l'écriture au féminin *(writing in-the-feminine), because* l'écriture féministe *is felt to point towards a content-oriented (and often narrowly political) interpretation of text. While, in English, the term "feminist writing" is preferred to "writing in-the-feminine," because, in our language "writing in-the-feminine" fails to invoke the assertive experimental note of female-gendered writing that the French* l'écriture au féminin *implies.*

In my women's writing group, we decided to take up the issue by writing essays in answer to the question: Qu'est-ce qui est incontournable dans le féminisme quand on écrit? *I, for one, imagine writing by feminists to be writing that cuts across the taboos not only of dominant ideology, but also those that arise as our feminist awareness attempts to structure new "meaning" for women. For me, consciousness, or "what I see" comes inevitably accompanied in writing by the temptation to transgress these very limits of vision through the play of language. Towards the "unfeminist" figure of melancholy, for example. That permeating contemporary melancholy of this decadent end-of-century which has to do with the seemingly hopeless destruction of* Mother Earth. *Whom we (at least white society) have treated as we often do our biological mothers: narcissistically, exploitatively.*

For, a writer may do as she pleases with her epoch. Except ignore it.

Qu'EST-CE QUI EST INCONTOURNABLE (Eng. trans: unskirtable!) dans le féminisme quand on écrit? I love that, the idea of one's feminist consciousness being **unskirtable,** i.e. untameable, unladylike . . . What of one's feminist consciousness is unskirtable in writing? "Honesty" comes my somewhat incongruous and intellectually unsatisfying answer. What? Does that mean one's feminist conscious keeps one honest? Or does it mean the opposite: that one's writing somehow transcends one's political commitment? "Honesty," I answer stubbornly, while in my mind, the feminist who wants positive, forward-looking models for women confronts the writer who envies Proust and Kafka. What does she envy? Their "freedom" to follow, in their fiction, the darker trails of being.

Fittingly, outside it is a grey November day. Through my window on Jeanne Mance St. is a suite of three-dimensional planes. The bare trees in the immediate foreground. Across the street, the rounded garrets, the fancy trim on top of the turn-of-the-century houses. Behind them a highrise building blocking out a portion of the sky. And to the left of that, tucked in a corner of the picture, the hump of mountain with its cross. That cross which reflects the present *slant*—shining absurdly bright up there as if melodramatically overstating a much-diminished power.

Arbitrarily, I choose this setting for my heroine. She's a writer who wants to explore the uncanny, maybe even delve into women's *tragic* potential. Except the word *tragic,* when traced (indirectly, on her computer screen) glitters with irony. Perhaps because classical tragedy's cause-and-effect narrative underscored patriarchal values. Or because it aspired to unary, all-powerful heroes, who wouldn't reflect her sense of self. Although, *elle a envie de vivre grande,* to cast shadows like Ozymandias on the sand. But . . . a female-sexed Oedipus? Grotesque. A feminine Hamlet? Closer, maybe. Still, there's something unsuitable (for her) about his relationship with his mother ...

Yet, it is precisely in the direction of those figures that she feels herself reaching. Reaching for something beyond the almost too-proper image of the "strong woman" of a certain kind of feminist fiction, marching with her sisters towards a better future. Reaching, of course, also beyond that other extreme of "women's fiction": the soapy harlequins, obsessed largely with the risks and perils of heterosexual love. (Albeit, that cry for love interests her, since it's "tragic" to she who utters it, but melodramatic to the surrounding culture.) Reaching, too, beyond the "objective" factors of oppression as expressed (hence trivialized) in the journalese of newspapers: *tragic* poverty; *tragic* accident; *tragic* rape and murder. Even if she recognizes them as surface signs of some deeper riddle in-the-feminine lurking in the human psyche; or of some remote error of this civilization that refuses to confront death—while wreaking it on the balance of the planet.

Defiantly, she reaches towards the uncanny, because to do so is the ultimate proof her own women's culture has come of age enough to trust her when she writes. But in that space beneath the mantle of courage, of bravery that women have worn for centuries, she'll find what?

1. In old movies, the tragic moment was often signaled by clouds amassing in the sky. Driving along the highway with huge, black moving clouds banking before the storm, one gets a terrible feeling of human emptiness. The mind casts about desperately for the source of discomfort. It may fasten on fear of an accident as the big raindrops start. As they begin hitting the windshield with greater and greater force. No, the mind knows this fear of an accident is really a projection of fear from a deeper source: fear of the uncanny. In a jigsaw puzzle, you take apart the clouds gathering angrily over the spacious park above the castle. AND YOU FIND NOTHING. This is both reassuring and terrifying.

2. Sitting, as a girl, on the verandah in the village where I grew up, the angry pink-black clouds were almost a temptation. Beside me, mosquitoes bit at my brother's neck causing huge, red welts. I was glad. I hated him. He was my Mother's favourite. I watched the storm whipping up the dust by the side of the road. Mother was standing behind my rocking chair. Her unhappiness was the turmoil in all our souls. Beyond our lawn, other dramas with no solution were being played out in our half Irish-Protestant, half French village with its red-brick houses and false-fronted stores. As the storm blew up, I imagined myself as the heroine of a "tragic" southern novel. I later cried through every minute of *Gone With The Wind*. Reveling... Actually, watching myself revel, as if there were an almost comic distance between me, the little girl, and the self participating in the "tragedy" of the story.

But here the narrator senses a painful dichotomy. On one hand she understands (i.e. grasps with her whole body) the need for the positive reaffirmation of female subject. In fact she remembers exactly the moment she grasped this completely. Summer, 1977, in Montréal. There were women on a lawn. Drinking sparkling wine. Their soft voices, their soft hair and women's skin seemed to waft through the air. One of them had written: *Women in space*. Meaning, of course, not women Astronauts. But women occupying space, now at last, as it spirals out before them. On some crazy, wild, maybe above all erotic, voyage to the future.

On the other hand, there was this pubescent identification with Scarlett O'Hara in *Gone With The Wind*. The little girl, the little Fury, was sitting on the verandah thinking of *herself* crying over *Scarlett's* life. Sitting there with her mother behind her, watching another mosquito dig its long delicious point expertly into the white neck of her brother. The first heavy raindrops made the dust on the road bounce up in lacy little circles. She hardly knew what *tragic* meant, but something drew her towards that dark place the word would come to represent.

Later, her empathies were more tangible, more serious: her friends, a mother with several children down the street abandoned by her husband, the war-torn women of Vietnam, feminists.... But still, she noted in a green notebook with white tulips embossed on the cover:

Woman has a narcissistic, almost masturbatory image of love
The image of the beloved is more precious than his presence

It was the morning after a love affair, and she was watching herself. Watching like the little Fury had watched (herself) cry over *Gone With The Wind*. That watched self becoming, then watching, other selves: the self that's critical, for example, of she who identifies with Scarlett; or of she who has just written in the new notebook in the museum of an art gallery. The watched selves opening out infinitely out like a Russian doll. Or like the hieroglyphics of the Russian futurist painter Popova, climbing in crooked lines across her work as if a score for urban music. To the left of a scene stands Stalin like a magnanimous cuckold.

In the gallery café, my heroine added to her notes in the green book:

Mon Héroine a envie de vivre grande.

Sensing that is where transgression starts.

Sensing also the gap between her grandiose desires and the nagging pain inside—that covered what?

Still, here's the "rub": isn't the contemporary feminist heroine meant to be a model of progress? Oedipus, apparently, was a loser: struck by Fate for killing Dad, the better to sleep with Mother. As for Hamlet, he "lost" (his sense of self, allegedly) because he couldn't choose between his mother and his father. His *To be or not to be* was a contemplation of suicide issuing from the depths of his existential despair (caused by the ultimate hidden fear that he was homosexual?).

A female heroine uttering the same phrase would more likely be contemplating everyday life. Her question being *To exist or not to exist* as speaking subject? A question to which a writer who's a feminist can only answer in the positive. *To be.* For to answer otherwise would be to shrink back into the chaos of nonsubject, into the clichés that have largely objectified her in patriarchal culture.

In women's novels of the 70s and early 80s, *To be* has been to kick and scrape our way out of the margins of patriarchy (the kitchen, the wife of the traditional heterosexual couple), "ascending" or sidestepping into historical space. Except, as Virginia Woolf already warned in *Three Guineas,* stepping into male "processions," (the professions of law, politics, "academia," for example) was dangerous because it had to be on male terms. So that *To be,* as woman, a subject in all her articulated difference, where her gestures might really match her words, could never be completely satisfied.

Another space of "being" in women's fiction is the Amazon utopia. This space, *unconditionally lesbian,* avoids the dilemma raised by Woolf—of trying to make it on patriarchal terms—by situating herself beyond history. In a space where she, the future-projecting Amazon, becomes ... almost a new female icon. But *utopia is an emotion,*[1] not necessarily psychically accessible to every writer. And my heroine, who's trying to create other heroines on her computer screen, also sees the Amazon (although admittedly attracted to her) as a self-proclaimed superior. As if the Amazon, in rising to her utopia, casts shadows not only on the ground, but also on other women.

So where then, and *how,* might my subject, denied her full existence in any patriarchal paradigm, yet not seeing herself as Amazon, *be* a subject-in-the feminine? That is, where and how in writing? If she (who, on the computer screen still appears in series, all the watched parts constantly coming apart, fitting together again...) cannot be expressed in any established form, she needs to find another place where the words she speaks will fit her gestures. A place as excessive as the Amazon's bold step outside history, yet, (she's a Capricorn) a place where her struggle for integrity might be more earthbound than the Amazon's utopia.

The heroine smiles. Maybe the Dark is just utopia inside out. Maybe the basic characteristic of writing from a feminist consciousness is simply that it cannot be reabsorbed into their processions—philosophically or in terms of form. But how, precisely, does a feminist consciousness frame this movement towards the excessive (the unlawful)? Without becoming law itself?

The little Fury looks at the brother sitting between her and her mother on the verandah while the stormclouds gather. The black clouds also remind the little Fury that she is afraid. What will happen after the thunder clap explodes? Will lightning strike the house? The mother sits with her lips pursed. Earlier that day, the little Fury heard her mother crying as she scrubbed the oak floor. She understood her mother was thinking how she wanted to leave them all and be a missionary in Africa.

But my heroine has paused to wonder why the little girl has become a little Fury on her computer screen. Has history finally come full circle? In the myth, Erinyes (the Furies) hounded Oedipus to death at Colonus in Attica. His crime? Perhaps society was punishing him for unconsciously trying to substitute the matrilineal for the patrilineal line. I like to think the Erinyes were furious at his failure. It's true that throughout history, they've always been somewhere in the picture: the witches, the suffragettes, and now the second-wave feminists. One of them, the little girl, sat on the verandah projecting herself into the mosquito (only the females bite) raising the welts on the neck of her brother. Yes, *Les Mouches* de Sartre. Negatively prophetic. The Erinyes, emerging again, maybe this time ready to upset the power on which the whole Oedipan drama is based. To uncover the matrilineal traces buried in the folds of classical drama. And expand them into new time, into the new space that opens before us as the law wavers on the edge of social, ecological disaster....

Perhaps this desire for that lost matrilineal consciousness explains the attraction of the Dark, the uncanny, for the little Erinys sitting on the verandah, listening to the buzz of mosquitoes. There is an ominous foreboding in the black stormclouds. But, that foreboding is also charged with eroticism. It occurs to my heroine looking at her computer screen that the doubleness of the little Erinys (that bittersweet mixture of eroticism and foreboding) might hold the clue to a new kind of heroine. A new heroine who is not merely the feminine of hero (*a name given to men of superhuman strength, courage, ability, favoured by the Gods*[2]). Nor heroine as it was implied in the 70s wave of anglo-American feminist criticism.[3] That is the (female) hero as a logical extension of nineteenth-century bourgeois notions of enlightenment (i.e., where light is reason, wielded by the highest forces of moral authority to conquer "darkness"). And by extension, also of Marxist ideology (inasmuch as the concept of total(itarian) victory of light over dark was synonymous with progress). In the latter paradigm, the (female) hero and his (her) kind must end up successful in their specific project, be it personal, professional or "revolutionary." For there can only be the victors and the victims, the former the subjects of progressive novels, the latter censored.

No, my heroine imagines a new heroine closer to an earlier meaning of the word: *At Delphi a[n] ... ascension ceremony conducted wholly by women was called the Herois, or 'feast of the heroine.*[4] And this ascension represented Persephone's cyclical rise from Hades, not to "heaven," but to wander *about on the earth with Demeter (her mother) until the time came for her to return to the Underworld.*[5] It is the notion of cyclical ascension, and descent (in contrast to the dominant pattern of linear rise to climax in patriarchal drama), that appeals to my heroine as she tries to work this all out on her computer screen. For this notion would permit her heroine (her set of heroines) to be both grandiose and humble, miserable and angry, not to mention any other imaginable contradiction, without shame . . .

Now, how exactly would this subject in writing be structured by her feminist consciousness? And why do I keep dancing around the issue as if to keep it at a distance?

In fiction, modernity was inadvertently involved in opening the space where a new female subject might emerge in all her difference. Inadvertently because modernity wanted to deconstruct the subject (the better to eliminate author-ity), yet in the space opened by this recognition of narrative-in-crisis (a crisis which feminist writers also strongly felt), a new subject-in-the-feminine emerged. Inadvertently, because male philosophers, in naming this new decoded space of writing "feminine" (*woman is neither truth nor non-truth for Derrida and is therefore akin to the spacing which is writing*[6]), tried to keep it "feminine" on their terms, i.e., insisting it not be used to assert female subjectivity. (Which feminists naturally perceived as tantamount to trying to keep the female subject down, under the space hidden by yet another male palimpsest.) Furthermore, the subject-in-the-feminine reconstituted in this space remains essentially multiple. (The Greeks sometimes thought of Persephone as triple: Diana in the leaves, Luna, shining brightly, Persephone in the Underworld.) The subject's resistance to drawing rigid boundaries around herself (she's herself, yet also somehow linked to other women—neither unary nor "deconstructed") *makes her incomprehensible to the male modernist*—and embarrassing.

But can this subject, like Persephone, admit to a cyclical retreat into shadow (whence Persephone was, according to the myth, at first, brutally abducted) and still be up to scratch from the feminist viewpoint?

It's a grey day. My heroine (the writer) is at her desk creating heroines. When, outside, suddenly appears the sun. So the three-dimensional plane of mountain, flat-topped roofs, and the balcony look black, in the shadow with the light coming from behind like the negative of a photo. This darkish place reminds her that Walter Benjamin once said photography made MAN realize he (too) could be objectified.[7] And Barthes noted how violent was the experience of becoming that photographic object: a "micro-experience" of death, he said. This led certain men to think they could understand how women felt stuck in a constant transitional gap between object / subject.[8]

Of course, the dark space in which man sees woman-the-object lurking isn't necessarily "dark" to her. In fact, it functions in reverse precisely as in the relationship between photo negative and print. What's "dark" (absence, gap) for him is something else for her. Lucidity, perhaps, inasmuch as she feels she exists as subject. A consciousness dependent, it would seem, on its links to the feminist community. Because it is the feminist community which has claimed her right *to be*, to exist body, mind, and creativity with some small degree of ... credibility. A locus where she might at last *have the impression* of living in the present (as opposed to a nostalgic past or a rose-coloured future created in some patriarchal image). Where she experiences the euphoria of discovering what it means to care for women. (That cliché about how you recognize a dyke in a bar: she's the one who looks you in the eye and LISTENS TO WHAT YOU'RE SAYING.) The surge of love for self and others caused by the touch of women's skin to women's skin; of rooms full of the music women's voices make. A locus that keeps the self from shattering or from distraction by the prerogatives of patriarchy coded into memory.

What happens when I start to write from this space of *herself-defined,* knowing this is the only space from which I can write forward? Will my act of writing be too contained within that circle of light where women are significant (i.e. where we have meaning)? Can I explore beyond it and still be "correct" politically? May I admit, like *The Princess and The Pea,* that despite all those mattress layers of solidarity provided by feminism, I cannot prevent myself from being conscious of a deep internal knot?

The writer looks out her window. Behind the three dimensional set (trees, roofs with their carved, almost Eastern-European decorations, and the mountain) the sky is grey. And getting greyer every minute, like that day she was driving down the highway with clouds banking furiously before a storm. When suddenly a terrible feeling of human emptiness. What does a feminist do with this? Her mind casts about for the source of discomfort. Patriarchy! The answer seems limited. As the big raindrops start, her mind fastens on the old fear of an accident. But the accident is only a projection of the fear coming from that unknown source. That source that can only be named: uncanny. In the jigsaw puzzle, you take apart the clouds gathering angrily over the spacious park of a French château. And you find nothing: you're confronted with yourself.

When confronted with himself, Hamlet conjured up his father. And his (cuckolded) father said: Do something about my honour. Which Hamlet interpreted as: do something about your mother and her lover, my usurper. But can a woman, when confronted with nothing, so easily conjure up her mother?

The rub for Persephone was that she had to live divided— half the year in the Underworld and half the year, on EARTH, where she wanted to be, with her mother. In this, unlike Hamlet, she was not ambivalent. It was her mother who was significant.

I think Persephone's story reflects something of what every woman writer who attempts to explore the "dark" is also getting at: her desire to reach (to grasp in language) the mother as a woman.[9] On the verandah, something about the odd presence of her mother kept the little girl fascinated. Although she didn't have the language to wonder why she seemed so distant (and at the same time so penetrating). Sometimes, she suspected it was because her brother was her mother's favourite. Surveying the welts on his neck, she was glad that he was so allergic to mosquitoes. The fact she was not allergic proved she was of a superior branch of nature. Later, her passionate love for Proust's writing was also tinged with jealousy. He seemed to have the right to expect his mother's kiss— something she never felt herself. She wrote in her notebook:

Proust's childhood anxiety about love was based on forcing mother's kiss.
A request always to be repeated because he couldn't have it freely.

It occurred to her that a woman writing a story such as Proust's, but with a female subject, would be considered weird for even wanting the kiss so much. Take Freud's Dora, whose attachment to her mother (and to her father's mistress!) earned her the label of hysteric. Hysteric in the sense of sick, overblown, a woman who made a nuisance of herself. Whereas Proust's hysteria became a miracle of beauty. Was this because he was a man, i.e., by gender, on the right side of culture? Or because of the magnificence of the writing—born in part of his "maladjustment," his *brisure* with what was expected sexually of a man?

To be or not to be, for a woman, would normally involve (in terms of identity) a movement towards the mother. Except the mother's presence in language has been reduced to utilitarian function (the mother is not a person). Making it difficult for the little girl to break the symbiotic hold of the relationship enough to see the woman in the mother. So the mother always seems partly in the shadow. Maybe that's why she ends up in my (and other women's) prose as a semi-Gothic character, a figure of *excess,* of *hope,* but also of terrible *absence.* Perhaps that relationship with her mother, which is, in part, the heroine's relationship with herself, is an element of the knot (the pea) felt by the princess under all those mattress layers. To be sure, feminism (her circle of women) displaces this disturbance in the process of attributing her, the emerging subject, meaning. One would think, also, that feminism would be open to exploring the darker side of being—given the mother's "place" in it. But, paradoxically, that positive image of the indomitably courageous feminist marching down a straight road towards the sun feels like a block when she, the writer, tries to reach, in a poetic gesture, towards the negative (cohabited by the muted mother, murdered species of all kinds, death in particular and in general). Because the feminist is almost a wall of meaning, meaning ... which *identified ... within the unity or multiplicity of subject ... guarantees transcendence, if not theology*[10].... Hence, in contradiction with the poet in her, who is also drawn elsewhere, towards *la séduction du glissement ... (laquelle est) celle-là même de la poésie, du fonctionnement poétique du langage.*[11] For where

else but in poetic language may she, the subject be inscribed
in all her (unnameable) complexity?

Outside my window a cold rain beats horizontally over the
stage set of flat-fronted houses, their tops varied with pretty,
fluted decorations. I'm writing about the mother who spent
her lifetime on a theological mission. She was trying to find
some ultimately perfect interpretation of the Bible, some true
meaning. Around her in the village, the Protestant sects
mocked her efforts with four different Churches (for a Protestant population of less than 300—the other three hundred
were French and Catholic). Yes, she made me suspicious of
transcendence, a suspicion that has led me to place myself (in
writing) between certain expectations of my feminist community and my desire to be excessive. In analysis, I've noticed, it's
often the areas of repression in the mind, the darkest corners,
that, if worked through, lead to fascinating places. Although
even the unconscious isn't innocent. Who knows how deep
one must go to free oneself of human nature's well-
conditioned tendency towards conventional thinking?

    1973: A far-left group in Québec which claims to support the
slogan All Freedom in Art. *Still, I'm complaining to a comrade*
about what I perceive as my lack of validation. He says you
have three strokes against you: You're English, you're a mother,
you're an artist. I joined up with some surrealists who were fel-
low travelers of our group. They were for "total revolution"—
the clue to which, they believed, lay in the unplumbed gold of
the latent content of our dreams. We also explored the uncon-
scious through collective sessions of automatic writing. But of
course, language never springs forth "pure." I seemed to sense
this more than the others who were mostly men. For from their
unconscious, "woman" always APPEARED as muse: as useful

object for "total revolutionaries" to use. And although the access I gained to unconscious material from this experience has always proved invaluable—the whole context was, for me, one in which it was impossible to invent myself—or any fiction—in writing.

Here, the matter of *what's unskirtable in our feminism* gains a nuance. That women's circle must be not only an ongoing presence that fosters the process of reinvention of her body in a language no longer reflected slant from the realm of patriarchal meaning. BUT, for it to work for her as artist, this women's circle must be propitious to (her) self-invention while resisting closure, i.e., the tendency to become, in its vision, a new convention.

The little girl also *tried to invent* herself each day. She'd step off the curb and write in her mind: *The little girl stepped off the curb*. She'd cross the street and write in her mind: *The little girl crossed the street*. But as she grew up and started having the usual gamut of relationships with men, her attempts at invention kept slipping out of focus. At the same time, she sensed a terrible ambivalence about the image society invented for her. It would burst forth unexpectedly, in the form of attacks on the weak flanks, on the vulnerable side her lovers showed in intimacy. As if she bore towards them an unabiding anger fed not by circumstances but by some deeper source. In horror the young woman atoned for her excesses by graciously learning to *defer*. By developing cool, offhand ways, (une belle indifférence?) to cover her fear that the *"body might do something inappropriate."* This warning about the body's potential inappropriateness had come to her from her father in a dream. A dream where, across the street, the pregnant silhouette of Mme. Cousineau was planting her garden under a full moon. While on their verandah, her husband did a mocking twostep.

Into this narrative, feminism came as a tremendous relief. But no sooner had she arrived in that warm and cozy place, than she wanted more: she wanted both the legitimizing community, and for that community to cast no moral judgements on the free flow of her desire, of her imagination. For the more radical she was (the more she wished to dangle dangerously on the edge of meaning) the more she, who exists only negatively in the symbolic, needed a frame within which to reinvent herself, *yet spin free.*

To ask so much understanding of community, she knew, was also to commit herself to intense engagement in it. How else to ascertain it be a place with a strong notion of being always in the process of *becoming.* So that it didn't make the mistake of more traditional progressive movements, limiting creative freedom by applying the shorter vision of politics. ("Your work isn't positive enough to be feminist," says a feminist writer from English Canada. "It doesn't show an upbeat enough image of solidarity." "But," I reply, at first feebly, then angrily. "It's about the relationship between thinking and feeling; about the struggle between *her* feminist consciousness—in both its greatness and its limitations—and social constructs, memory, dreams, nightmares.") No, her feminist community must be adventurous enough to admit that language is more than meaning: it is also music. Music, as our bodies themselves are rhythm, music, so long distorted, muted.

Male writers, too, have highlighted the importance of the fact that the body constantly reinvents itself in speaking. *Un corps,* says Lacan ... *c'est de la parole comme telle qu'il surgit.*[12] But in her case, the *parole* is coded by the dominant culture to despise the body from which it springs.... Indeed, the very vastness of the gap, between her desire for selfhood and her relationship to language in patriarchal culture, may point, for some, to the source of "tragic" in her. However, it's interesting to note that this (patriarchal) "tragedy" cannot be transposed to her without its meaning slipping. For the tragic moment in the classic sense occurred when the hero (perhaps unwittingly) finally *closed* the gap between his words and acts (bodily performance)—by recognizing (he had failed) patriarchal law.[13] In other words, it occurred when word (usage), body and law came into line. Hamlet became a tragic figure—came to his point of no-return—when he verbally acknowledged what his problem was: (that he was a (homosexual?) traitor in terms of patriarchal values). For Oedipus, it was when he was forced to recognize (verbally again) that he was the very father-murderer his own words had so drastically condemned.

But she, the heroine, cannot close that gap between word (usage), body and the father's law, unless she becomes a parody of herself (a little man). Or a fragment (the cliché of mother, lover, prostitute). Yes, the "tragic" gap for her could only be closed by her acceptance of reduced representation of her body (self) in society, i.e., with absurdity. (Hamlet's problem, multiplied.) Conversely, the more she wills herself to speak, the more alienated she finds herself from the father's word. Until she realizes the "tragic" gap is so great, so disastrous it's almost comical. Until she sees (at least if she's a feminist) that her words can never be in line with both her body and the father's law at the same time. That she doesn't want them to. She'll never be Oedipus, or Hamlet. Her words will take her elsewhere. But where? Towards the mother? Here, I think, begins the real tragic journey. For it's more complex than that: it's a double-sided journey, now towards her, now towards him (i.e. culture).

It will take the strength of her and all her sisters to write through this dark, confusing place without tipping the balance to psychosis. That's why the spectacle (the performance) of herself, in which she leaps right through the layers of patriarchal "meaning" that cover her presence in this world often has the distancing humour of a carnivalesque dance. That's why the body, her body, which by its very leap transgresses, as it moves beyond cognizance towards excess, towards the danger zones spawned by dreams, feeling, memory, holds very tightly to the hand of her sisters. Sisters who like her see a tremendous future in inscribing the dialectics of subject (the tension between thinking and feeling, for one). Instead of setting up moral constructs to frame her writing (as in the traditional novel). Traditional forms cannot speak the pluralist language of her spectacle. At any rate, like Virginia Woolf, she's bored with narrative.

> *Also, why not invent a new kind of play:*
> *Woman thinks . . .*
> *He does.*
> *Organ plays.*
> *She writes.*
> *They say:*
> *She sings.*
> *Night speaks.*
> *They miss.*[14]

She looks out the window, at the harsh grey light shining on the round or pointed pediments that give those flat rooftops an Eastern cast, thinking she has (arbitrarily) chosen the right setting for her heroine(s). Because the strip of light on the pediments topping the buildings across the street, is, in its relationship to the night, rather like the image she has always had of her women's circle: a slightly lit-up point in a dark place; a spot of laughter in fact *slanting* off the back of tragedy. What better way to span that distance between "self" and mother (identity), "self" and father (culture), than with an ironic smile or hoot of laughter? A sense of (black) humour that carries with it, that glitters with the whole weight of the tragedy that surrounds it.

Yes, there's something carnivalesque about the way she is. Something carnivalesque about the polyphonic voices that

move through her stories—since she's not the Amazon, flying
high, but down there on the darkening earth (in these reactionary, polluted, warlike times) with people from many
walks of experience and privilege (although intimately pro-
tected by her women's circle). And in her insistence on being
always in a process of becoming (i.e. in refusing to see things
as binary opposites like "good – bad," even "masculine – feminine" as much as she refuses closed endings, fixed meanings), in all of these things, she thinks her new "narrative"
might have something of the ambivalence and excess of carnival.

Yet, I don't want to overstate this carnival figure. It may be
carnivalesque in its conscious distancing from culture's
definition, containment of us. (We know that uttering our sins
as Hamlet did, as Oedipus, won't help: we can't erase the
body's "inappropriateness.") The better to mock the insult.
Except, whereas carnival in both the modern and classic
sense, seems to imply the dissolution of the subject into the
frenzy of the parade, her carnival is a performance of subjects
of a new sort. Subjects which, it's true, keep dividing into
actor, spectator.[15] But divide to recompose again, for each
subject's eye reflects other female likenesses profoundly—be
they rich, poor, "straight," lesbian, "visible" minority or not. In
this version of the carnival, the emphasis is not on the decadence of this historical period, where the disintegration of the
subject passes for progressive. Rather, she and her sisters are
dressed up for the explosion (the end of the era) in robes of
stunning irony: obsessed with understanding the gap
between their feminism and the physiological residue of
experience (battering, childbearing, love, nuclear waste . . .
which also have their truths); obsessed with the pull between
ideology and the unconscious, between the mask (a slant
attempt at synthesis of meaning) and the laughter that in the
same breath assures transgression: *" . . . l'humour . . . n'int-
ervient, fort souvent, que pour subvertir, pour remettre en question, ou pour mettre en suspens, le savoir."*[16]

She knows this tragi-comic act is not the only fictional performance possible on this stage / street leading towards the future. It is only one way of indicating the widening breach of History; it is only her current angle on these (postmodern?) times (where certain male philosophers and writers see death, while women imagine, rather, the death of patriarchy). And what's honestly unskirtable about her feminism is that it only structures the cognizant part of now, is hence only the first step on the path leading towards tomorrow. There will be other fictions, other theories, other utopias. But just now, she the feminist, she the artist, is in her third-floor apartment getting dressed in her robes of ambivalence, in her mask which is a comment on her current grasp of meaning, to go and join the carnival below.

Montréal, 1988

NOTES

1 Nicole Brossard (spoken at an organizing meeting of the International Feminist Book Fair, October, 1987).

2 The Compact Edition of the Oxford English Dictionary.

3 I am thinking of the kind of criticism that often appeared in militant feminist periodicals of the 70s and early 80s, where books were judged politically "correct" according to certain criteria: a woman must be "strong," not a "victim," etc., although exactly what was meant by those terms varied greatly according to the critic.

4 Robert Graves, *Greek Myths* (London: Cassell, 1965), p. 110.

5 Ibid, p. 111.

6 From Alice Jardine's reading of Jacques Derrida's *Spurs: Nietzsche's Styles / Epérons,* in ch. 9 of *Gynesis* (Ithaca: Cornell University Press, 1986).

7 Walter Benjamin "La photographie," in *Poésie et révolution* (Paris: Denoel, 1971).

8 Roland Barthes, *La chambre claire* (Paris: Editions du Seuil, 1980), esp. pp. 30-31.

9 Louise Dupré set me thinking along these lines when she said, at one of the meetings of our writing group: "Le drame, c'est qu'on ne peut jamais atteindre la mère." Lise Weil also touches on it in her unpublished dissertation on Virginia Woolf and Christa Wolf.

10 Julia Kristeva, *Desire In Language: A Semiotic Approach to Literature and Art,* trans. Léon S. Roudiez, Alice Jardine and Thomas Gora (New York: Columbia University Press, 1980), p. 124.

11 Soeren Kierkegaard, cited by Shoshana Felman, *Le Scandale du corps parlant* (Paris: Editions du Seuil, 1980), p. 170.

12 Cited by Felman, op. cit., p. 129.

13 This, as I mentioned in "Spaces   Like   Stairs," is an articulation of Felman's (*La source du tragique consiste non dans l'acte, mais dans la rencontre ... entre l'acte et le langage*), p.130.

14 Virginia Woolf, *A Writer's Diary* (New York: Harcourt Brace Jovanovich, Inc., 1953), p. 103.

15 Kristeva, op. cit., p. 78.

16 J.L. Austin, cited by Felman, op. cit., p. 171.

JOSÉE LAMBERT

GAIL SCOTT grew up in a bilingual community in Eastern Ontario and now lives and writes in Montreal. She was a journalist for several years, writing about Québec culture and politics for the *Montreal Gazette* and *The Globe and Mail*. Her books *Spare Parts* and *Heroine* were published by Coach House Press. She has also published in the anthologies: *La Théorie, un dimanche, Fatal Recurrences, A Mazing Space*, and *In The Feminine*. She is co-founder of *Spirale*, a French-language cultural magazine, and *Tessera*, a bilingual periodical of feminist criticism and new writing.